Civilian War

Civilian War

Bill Pank

Contents

To my RVing family, Marie, Allison, and Kealey. We've travelled many miles and seen so much together. I've loved every minute of it. I couldn't have asked for better traveling companions.

Print ISBN 979-8-9904189-0-5

E-Book ISBN 979-8-9904189-1-2

First Printing, 2024

1

∽

July 1 - Near Calgary, Alberta - morning

What sounded like dozens of birds just outside the camper woke Jim up. As he slowly gained consciousness, he felt like it was quite early to be waking up on the first day in almost a month that his family had nothing planned and no place to go. He cracked open one eye to get a sense of the time and could tell by the quality of the light that it was well before the time he had intended to start his day. Slowly, with as little movement as possible, he reached out to grab his phone off the counter by the bed and checked the time – 5:11 – even earlier than he expected. *What do the birds have to be singing about at this time of day? Why do they need to be so loud, so early?* Joy and the girls were likely to stay in bed until 7:30 or 8:00, so he should either try to get back to sleep or slip out quietly and stay out for a couple of hours. Maybe he should go out and scare away the birds so they don't wake up his wife.

They had been living in a thirty-foot motorhome for over three weeks now and Jim had gotten plenty of practice getting out of bed without disturbing everybody else's sleep, but one wrong move and the whole camper would be rocking like a ship in a storm. As he did nearly every morning, Jim lamented that he couldn't have bought a more expensive model of RV that had built-in, electronic leveling and stabilizers for camping, but they had always been a family that was on the go on their vacations, never in one place for more than a night's sleep, and pricy options like electric stabilizers and slide-outs were not a good use of the family budget. The solar panels and satellite dish he installed this spring had come in handy recently, but there were lots of other extras and up-grades he would love to have right now. Given the current circumstances, he wondered if he would make different decisions if he had a do-over – maybe he would be better off having a huge loan against the RV right now (good luck to the bank trying to collect on the loan or repossess the vehicle), and maybe all the money he saved in his retirement account wasn't going to be there for his family after all. Then again, maybe they wouldn't have made it to this point if he had been driving a big class A, with a car towed behind it. *Stop spinning over and over about the same old stuff you can't control. Time to get up and out, as delicately as possible.*

He took a quick peek over his shoulder to make sure Joy was still sleep-ing then gingerly rolled out of the bed onto his toes. The thermometer hanging on the wall showed it was in the mid 60's outside, so he grabbed some shorts and socks, got the keys off the hook on the wall, slipped his phone and keys into the pocket of his shorts, and tiptoed out of the bed-room. As he snuck past the bathroom and kitchen areas of the camper, he decided against grabbing something to drink from the fridge and just kept going. In the living/dining area, he took a long look down at Alex, who was curled up in a sleeping bag on the fold-out sofa. He wasn't worried about waking her up with noise, she was Deaf and the most talented sleeper in the family. She would be the last one to wake up this morning, as she always was. Her twin sister, Kelly, on the other hand, was likely to wake up no matter how carefully Jim pulled off his exit. She was up in the sleeping area over the driver's cab and the only sound Jim could hear coming from that area right now was the sound of a fan, but Kelly was a light sleeper who tended to have a bad reaction when Jim woke her up too early – especially lately.

Jim picked up his shoes near the door and delicately tiptoed down the three steps to exit the camper. The door was the worst part. There was almost no way to open and close the camper door without making noise and shaking the RV. He got out as delicately as he could, shut the door as gently as humanly possible, and stepped into the clear, Canadian morning.

It was the kind of morning that traveling in an RV was made for and it made Jim think of all the national parks in the U.S. and Canada that they had camped in over the years. As the early riser in the family, he liked to get out and explore their immediate surroundings in the peaceful early morning hours while his family rested. This was no national park. There were no natural wonders to find just beyond the campground, but it was a beautiful morning for a walk, and it wouldn't be a bad idea to get familiar with the place in case they decided to stay here a little longer than the two nights they paid for. They had pulled in last night right around sunset and Jim was too tired after a full day of driving to do much more than the minimum hook ups needed to get them through the night – electricity and the crappy, manual stabilizers he propped up under the rear bumper (for all the good they did).

Jim quickly put on his shorts, socks, and shoes, then looked down to see exactly what he was wearing. The khaki shorts and green Minnesota Wild t-shirt he had worn to bed were a presentable enough combination for an early morning walk through a campground where he was unlikely to run into any Rockefellers or Trudeaus. From his memory of the map of the facilities he received at check-in, the campground had three loops. His RV was in the first loop, loop A, closest to the entrance, and he thought he could walk all three loops in about 30 to 40 minutes taking it nice and slow. Locking the RV door behind him, he started down the driveway, and turned right onto the campground road. Within a minute of starting his walk, he stopped abruptly and muttered "oh crap" just loud enough to be audible. The realization that he's about to walk through a Canadian campground wearing a t-shirt for an American NHL team, and the fact that it might bring some unwanted attention, has him rethinking his campground exploration. If there's anything that almost all Canadians know, it's hockey, and anyone who is up and about is going to figure out he's an American and probably want to talk to him about the situation on that side of the border. He's had enough of those conversations with well-meaning Canadians over the last few weeks and would like to avoid having any of them this morning. After weighing the risks of going back inside to change his shirt – no way he could pull that off without disturbing Kelly and Joy - against the likelihood of encountering other campers, he decided against going back. It's early, so there shouldn't be too many other campers on the road. "Ah, screw it," he grunted and continued on.

The campground seemed almost fully booked. There were very few unoccupied spots. This probably shouldn't have been surprising since it was Canada Day and most people would be taking the holiday off from work. He tried to see where the other campers were from based on their license plates and the plates he could see were mostly British Columbia, Alberta, or Ontario. *No U.S. license plates so far.* Was he hoping to find some other Americans or hoping there weren't any here? He wasn't sure himself and wouldn't know until he encountered some. He hadn't spoken to anyone from the U.S. since they went to check on Carl in Winnipeg on June 7th. That seemed like a long time ago now.

On the back end of loop C, he came across an older man sitting in a camp chair in front of an older Fifth-wheel attached to an equally old pickup truck. The man looked to be getting some fishing gear ready. Normally, Jim would offer a hearty greeting and maybe even start a conversation, depending on the receptiveness of the person he met. This morning he adjusted his path to the far side of the road away from the man's camp site, offered a cursory nod and "good morning" and kept walking. The man wished him a Happy Canada Day and looked like he wanted to say more, but Jim just waved, picked up his walking speed, and quickly got out of range.

The rest of the campground was still at rest and by the time Jim had worked through all of loops B and C and most of loop A, he figured the other campers must be resting up so they could stay up late for fireworks and celebration tonight. Just three years ago his family enjoyed a decent fireworks display on Canada Day near Saskatoon. He didn't feel much like celebrating today and hoped they were far enough outside of town that there wouldn't be too much noisy revelry. Fireworks might make the girls uncomfortable this year. For a few minutes he was lost in thought, thinking about how his girls loved to watch the July 4th display back in Duluth. *Is anyone going to be celebrating Independence Day this year? You could probably get a good seat at Bayfront without having to fight the usual crowds. It's unlikely anyone who works in city government could show their face out there to run the festivities though.*

As he pondered, he passed the entrance to the campground and was on the home stretch back to his site. He was less than fifty feet from his camper and could see the front of his RV when a voice from a campsite across the road from the driveway to his own campsite said, "Minnesota, huh?"

Looking to his left up the driveway, he could see an older white Prius with a small teardrop camper behind it, but no sign of the where the voice came from. The Prius had Oregon plates.

Scanning the campsite carefully, Jim slowly started walking up the drive towards the camper. Then he saw the source of the voice. At the back of the campsite was a hammock holding a man who Jim guessed would have been in his mid to late 30's with shoulder length hair. The man was holding a thick book, possibly a Bible.

"Yep, I'm from Minnesota," Jim started, "looks like you're from Oregon, is that right?"

The man didn't attempt to get out of the hammock, he lowered his book and replied, "Portland area. I'm Chad. Where in Minnesota?"

"Duluth. Right at the tip of Lake Superior. Nice to meet you Chad, I'm Jim." Jim kept a good thirty feet of distance from the hammock.

Chad then did a little roll and thrust his legs up and out of the hammock, got what seemed like a little bit of airtime, and landed on his feet. It reminded Jim of a child jumping off a swing. It was a maneuver that seemed well practiced and graceful. Jim thought he would have landed on his face trying to pull it off.

Chad dropped the book into the empty hammock – it was definitely a Bible – and cut the distance between them in half. "I went to school with a guy from Two Harbors. He talked about going to Duluth for concerts and shopping and meeting girls. Made it sound like a pretty cool place. You like it there?"

Chad was a bit taller than Jim, average build, and giving off a bit of a hippie/surfer vibe. He was driving that old Prius and staying in a small, one-person camper that couldn't have much in the way of amenities inside. It was the kind of camper that is used for sleeping, but not much else, by people who go camping to spend their time in the outdoors. It wasn't the type of camper you normally saw in an RV park and that piqued Jim's curiosity a bit. Plus, the guy was American, so they definitely had some shared interests there these days. Jim decided to just go with the flow and see where the conversation went. The guy seemed earnest. "Yep, I love living in Duluth. Good schools, not too big, good people, and plenty to do. I really hope we can go back there at some point."

Chad pointed towards Jim's RV. "I saw you out there last night with your daughter helping you get your camper set up. Does she know what's going on?"

Jim took a long, deep breath. "That's more than I want to get into right now. I don't even know what's going on back in Duluth right now. I'm here with my wife and daughters. We're all together and healthy. For now, that's blessing enough."

Chad nodded. "Fair enough, wasn't trying to pry. I don't have kids and don't know how I would be dealing with everything if I had to look out for more than just myself. Lucky for you that you were up here when things went to hell. When did you leave Duluth?"

Jim was expecting this question, knew the answer was going to get a reaction, and was interested to see exactly what that reaction would be. "June 6th, we left mid-morning and crossed the border late that evening."

Chad stared at him for a long time, his mouth wide open. The reaction was of someone who thought he knew exactly how difficult that trip from Duluth to the Canadian border was and wasn't sure he believed it was possible to have done it. Slowly recovering, all he could offer was, "How did you pull that off?"

"We had a lot of help and more luck than I can believe, even thinking about it now. My rig took a beating, but nothing fatal. You can come take a look at it later if you want to. From this distance you can't really tell how much duct tape I used to cover up the damage. It still needs some body work. Some parts had to be replaced, but there are lots of RV service places in Manitoba."

Jim decided to turn the conversation around at this point. "So, you must have crossed the border earlier than us. How long have you been in Canada?"

Chad seemed a little deflated for a second, he seemed to really want to hear the details of Jim's travels. Then he perked right back up again. "I got wind of what was about to go down on the evening of June 2nd and was on my way north first thing the next morning."

"Wait. What." Jim was stammering, anger starting to build up. "You knew what was going to happen four days ahead of time and instead of doing something to stop it, you ran for Canada?!!" Not quite yelling, but his voice was rising in volume and urgency. "We lost people getting out. I don't know if my mom or sister are alive. My kids have been through shit nobody should have to go through. Who knows how many people are dead and how many more have had their lives ruined. AND YOU KNEW ABOUT IT DAYS IN ADVANCE!" His fists were clenched now, and he was close to losing control.

Chad backed up a few paces and held his hands up palms out. "Whoa, whoa, whoa, it's not like that. Let me explain what went down before you blame me for everything. Man, I tried, my friends tried, even after I left my friends kept trying, but nobody who could do anything wanted to stop what was coming."

Jim cut him off, "Back up. How did you know on June 2nd that things were going to go bad?"

"It's going to take a little bit of explaining, you know. How about we sit down and I'll give you the whole story." He turned and started walking toward the Prius. "Do you want a bottle of water? I'm going to be thirsty." Chad popped open the back door of the car and grabbed a couple of bottles of water from a cooler.

They sat down across from each other with their waters and Chad started talking.

"So, I know some people around Portland who don't mind mixing it up in the streets with the Neo-Nazis, white nationalist types, and fascists. My friends were really busy for a while after the BLM protests when the white power groups decided to make a show of force, and somebody had to stand up to them. I'm guessing since you're here, you don't belong to any of those groups on either side. I'm no street fighter, but I believe in the cause and help out in other ways. I'm single and own my own house, so sometimes that means having a group of the guys over to make plans or just hang out. June 2nd was one of those days. Five of the guys came over to drink a few beers. They weren't planning anything, it was just a chance to spend some time with the guys. One of the guys brought a streaming device so they could watch a baseball game on my TV. This was not a bunch of subversives planning to take down the government. I mean, my friends don't care for the people running the country right now, but they're only focused on fighting the militias and fascists who are intimidating our neighbors. Never anything bigger than protecting our streets from the thugs. But, like I said before, that night wasn't about that. It was just the good guys getting away from their wives and kids for a few hours to hang out with their buddies."

Jim showed he understood. "Okay. So you support an Antifa group in your free time, but you don't take part in the violence. I'm with you. Keep going."

2

∾

June 2 - Outside Portland

Steve, a guy in his late 20's, who clearly finds the time to spend in the gym is just about through with his 2nd beer of the evening. As much as the group has a leader, Steve's charisma and personality have made him a sort of defacto leader of their small group. He and Chad have been having a friendly debate about how each of them thinks the changing climate will impact their lives. Chad's outlook is less dark, and Steve thinks that's because he doesn't have kids. Steve thinks the planet will be a total wreck in his kids' lifetimes, but that he won't be around to see it because he's going to be killed in the streets by the fascists, or the Feds, way before the climate can kill him. Neither of them has ever read an article in a scientific journal, so the debate is based on what little they've picked up from various news sources and modern media.

"How can you have not seen *The Day After Tomorrow*?" Steve was yelling good-naturedly. "It's like the quintessential climate emergency movie of our time."

Chad shook his head. "Didn't everybody in that movie have to go south to save themselves? I think the current predictions are that everything south of Portland is going to be a desert and we're all going to be farming Greenland in fifty years. That movie had me really confused. They need to pick one direction or the other."

Steve laughed. "Guess we better have go-bags packed for either scenario. Hope the climate can hold on until the President's war with the cartels ends or none of us is going to survive very long going south."

Jeff, a bearded, 40-ish, former marine, who scared the hell out of anyone who crossed him, but was a respected group leader, was standing unnoticed a few feet away. It was unusual for him to speak unless his input was necessary, so he surprised them with a contribution. "I really hope everyone has to go south. I want to watch some of our so-called friends try to beg and plead their way into Mexico. If we have to go north, those Canadians are so damn nice they'll just let all of those assholes in for humanitarian reasons." The last two words had a sarcastic tone. "Making those bastards skulk through the desert and sneak across the border into Mexico would be so damn satisfying. It would suck to lose our country, though."

Outside of planning for a mission, training for a mission, or as needed within the execution of a mission, nobody in the room had heard Jeff put that many words together consecutively before, so the whole place fell silent for about thirty seconds other than the play by play of the baseball game that was on the TV across the room. Then Steve spoke quietly. "Amen brother, but we'll fight those fuckers no matter where they go – North, South, East – I don't care where, I just want my kids to live in a free country."

While he was talking, Steve's phone started to vibrate. He looked down at it as he finished speaking and muttered, "Now who the hell is this," then pushed back from the table as he took the call. Since the room was already quiet, the guys watched Steve and listened in to his side of the call. "Yeah?.....Who is this?.......How did you get this number?.....Wait, say that again but slower........And I should take your word for this why?.....Bullshit, there's no way to organize something like that in secret.......Even if I believed you, I don't have the manpower to cover that much ground......Look man, you need to contact the Feds, I'm not looking to get my guys killed.....Hey, you still there?" He looked at his phone and could see the call was gone.

Since he already had everybody's attention, he filled in the blanks for the rest of the group. "Okay, I'm not sure exactly who that was and what group he's with, but I think it was one of those Three Percenters. Don't know how he got my number and that makes me a little bit uncomfortable, but that's an issue for later. He claims that some big shit is going to go down in the next few days, and not like street protest type shit, but take down the power grid and start executing people in the confusion type shit. He said it wasn't just Portland, but other cities too. He couldn't, or wouldn't, tell me exactly when and where they were planning to hit the grid, yet he wants us to do something about it. He said the Feds know about it and aren't going to do anything and those orders are coming from the White House through the DOJ. He's got to be full of it, right? There's no way the government is going to let a bunch of militias wreck the country even worse and kill a bunch of people, is there?"

They all looked at each other for about a minute in silence. Jon, who had been on the couch watching the baseball game before the call came in, spoke first. "I don't know. The President cleaned house in the DOJ and the FBI. Anyone there now is loyal to him. There might still be people there who would want to put a stop to throwing the country into total anarchy, but what are the chances they draw attention to themselves. I just don't think a conspiracy as big as you're talking about could be kept secret for long. This administration leaks like crazy. If more than five people in this government know something, it's on CNN within hours. Somebody's either pranking us or trying to get us exposed so they can hit us."

Steve looked around. "Anybody else have an opinion?"

Chad spoke up now. "If there's any chance this guy is telling the truth, we've got to get the word out to every Fed, sheriff's office, and police department we can. Is there a way we can do it anonymously so it can't get traced back to us? Hell, maybe that's this guy's deal, try to get us in trouble for falsely reporting."

Matt, the youngest member of their group, and generally considered the most tech-savvy jumped in. "Look, if they were planning this in any of their chat rooms, we'd already know about it. These guys have not done quiet planning well in the past. If they really are planning to start a purge and nobody knows about it, they must be doing it offline. We should contact people we know who have access to their message boards and chat rooms and have them post stuff about preparations for this big attack. Someone in law enforcement will see those posts and have to do something."

Steve thought it over. "Alright, Matt you reach out to everyone you know who has infiltrated their dark recesses on the web. And try to find some people who can figure out how to post anonymous tips to every online law enforcement tip line up and down the West Coast. Jeff, can you contact anyone you know who is still in the military and give them a heads-up on what might be coming? Maybe law enforcement and the military are already on top of this and is going to stop them before any-thing serious happens. Just in case, the rest of us need to call everyone in our contacts and tell them to be ready for action. Things could get really ugly and we don't want any of our friends caught with their pants down."

Everybody picked up their phones and started making calls.

3

July 1 - Outside Calgary - early morning

"So we made phone calls all evening and into the early morning. Around 1 a.m. everybody left to get their families ready for what might be coming. Jeff had a cabin way off the grid that runs on solar and is stocked for the end of the world. Some of the guys were going to send their wives and kids to stay there. I stayed up most of the night packing my car and getting my camper ready to roll. I didn't tell Steve I was going to make a run for it, but I think he knew.

When he left my place that morning, he said he hoped to see me again someday and asked that I look out for his family if he didn't make it. I called him on the 4th after I got to Vancouver and he told me it was still quiet, but he was sure something was about to happen. He had put out the word to our friends to buy as much ammunition as they could, and the people he heard back from couldn't find any. Every shop in the Portland area was sold out of anything useful. That convinced him. He sounded tired and nervous. He'd heard back from friends who had tried to warn the authorities and only some of the local cops were even interested in the information. The county sheriffs and the Feds blew off the warnings or were outright hostile to the messengers. He sent his family somewhere safe on the morning of the 4th, but he sounded like he thought this was going to be the end for him. Steve was a guy who had been in a lot of fights, but as far as I know, he hadn't killed anyone, and I suspect the idea of having to kill or be killed was weighing on him."

"I was able to reach Jeff on the 5th. I wanted to know if he had any luck with his military contacts. He doesn't normally show much emotion unless he's yelling at someone for messing up their assignment, but he was really upset. I didn't follow all of the technical jargon he used, but from what I could understand, one of his buddies, who is some level of officer, told him there was no chance his units would be deployed to protect civilians from other civilians. Since the U.S. went to war on the Mexican cartels, the military has been stretched thin with all the cartel's terrorist attacks in the border states and the humanitarian crisis down there. That's the priority from the top. Jeff said he thought the U.S. military was gearing up to invade Mexico any day now. He was cursing about the top brass, that they knew what was going to happen and were intentionally standing down. Their commander in chief wanted retribution against the people who had not supported him and was going to send the military into another country while his supporters took out that retribution on his own citizens. Jeff was sure that some troops would go AWOL to defend their families, but others would probably join in the siege. Hard to imagine, two guys who fought together in Iraq or Afghanistan, watching each other's backs overseas, come home and then they're facing off against each other over an American city. I really hope Jeff is still out there fighting right now and leading the resistance somewhere."

Chad paused and took a drink. "I tried calling Steve again on the 6th, but the call wouldn't go through. I haven't heard from anyone I know in the U.S. since the 5th. If I had to guess, some of my friends are dead by now and all of them have been fighting bad guys."

Jim's anger dissipated. He could sympathize with Chad's situation. Hadn't his first instinct been to get to Canada as well? He wished he had advance warning like the group in Portland, and if he didn't have a family, he liked to think he would have stayed and fought, but who knows. He wasn't in a position to judge Chad for his decisions and actions. Besides,

Chad just might be able to provide more information about the situation that could be helpful down the road. Jim had learned quite a bit from this conversation. Plus, Jim decided he kind of liked the guy. They probably wouldn't be attending baseball games and barbeques together, not that there would be any American baseball in the near future, but he wouldn't have any problem hanging out and talking with Chad a few more times while they were in the same campground.

He looked at his phone and saw it was almost 8:00. "I need to go check in with my family. Are you sticking around this place for a while?"

"Yeah. I've got this spot reserved for another 4 nights. I'm doing some odd jobs around here in trade for the spot, but the owner gave me the holiday off."

"Well, if you don't mind, I'll stop by later to talk some more."

"I wouldn't mind that at all. Stop by any time. I'm not going anywhere."

Jim got up. "Alright. See you later. Happy Canada Day."

4

June 6 - Duluth, Minnesota - around 1 a.m.

The complete lack of sound in the room woke Jim up with a start. *The fan was blowing when I came to bed.* He opened his eyes and noticed the room was in complete darkness. Not even so much as the glow of the nightlight in the girls' bathroom across the hall. The power was out.

5

May 17th - Duluth, Minnesota

Jim was nearly giddy sitting in the back of the Uber on his way to the RV shop. He was putting more than a few dollars into making his rig more self-sufficient and now it was finally ready to go. Josh met him at the service counter and explained the extensive charges on the invoice. While it was a good chunk of money, Jim gladly handed over his credit card. They went outside to the RV and Josh carefully walked Jim through the new bells and whistles of the solar charging system and the touch panel that he could use to monitor the batteries and the power being generated or used at any given time. Although the system didn't have enough power to run the camper's rooftop air conditioning unit, it could power just about everything else without having to plug into a shore line or run the generator. Now the family could be off grid for as long as their water supply held out and their waste tanks weren't overflowing. It wasn't like they could be completely self-sufficient. They still would have needed to plug in during that night they spent in Death Valley when the temperature outside never dropped below 100 degrees, but now they could run fans and plug in all their chargers during an overnight at a Walmart or anywhere else they camped off the grid. He wished he had installed the system before their trip to Alaska a few years back.

The other new addition was a satellite dish so they could access the internet from anywhere – even while they were moving. The dish came with one-year of service and Josh helped him get it set up so he could add devices to the system later. Jim wasn't sure he would renew the subscription after the first year, but he wanted it for this summer since they had a long trip planned for late June to Newfoundland and Labrador. Who knows what kind of cell service is available way up there. With the solar power and satellite internet, Jim was hoping his kids could watch some Disney+ on the big TV while they were on the road to pass some of those long driving days when kids can get impatient. In the four big trips they had taken in this RV, the TV had been used maybe three times. The new systems should change that and make it easier for the family while on the road. Jim plugged a Fire Stick into the TV and between the two of them they figured out how to get it linked to the Wi-Fi from the satellite dish.

After about an hour with Josh, Jim thought he knew enough to run both systems, so he thanked Josh for all his help and got ready to head home more excited than ever about how these new additions were going to make this year's vacation even better for his family. Before leaving the RV shop, Jim turned on the TV and found a baseball game to listen to during the drive home. Although he couldn't see the TV from the driver's seat (it hung from a swivel arm directly above and just behind him in the over the cab sleeping area), that was one of the most enjoyable baseball games he'd ever watched.

He couldn't wait to get home and take the kids for a little test drive while they watched a show. They probably wouldn't be all that impressed, because they were used to technology working everywhere and having every bit of knowledge and every person they know accessible at all times. As much as he and Joy liked to tell them about the days when there were four TV channels (with shows that you didn't watch on demand), no public internet, no GPS to guide you, and no phones in our pockets, the girls didn't seem to internalize what it was like to function in those times. They may as well have been explaining the Civil War era, for how unreal those stories seemed to the kids.

As he drove, Jim thought about the time he and Joy went to Los Angeles in the before times. They had rented a car at the airport and bought paper maps for Joy to use to navigate as Jim drove them around. If ever there was a technology that saved marriages, Jim thought it was GPS navigation. They never did find the Hollywood sign on that trip although that was one of the places on their to-do list. If they had GPS back then, they most likely would have driven right to it and would have spoken much more kindly to each other along the way. Now they've travelled in an RV to forty-nine states and eleven Canadian Provinces and Territories without so much as a raised voice at each other about how to get from one place to the next. Jim may have raised his voice at the GPS more than a few times over all of those miles, but Joy was no longer the target. In Joy's defense, she was born with low vision and was legally blind, so map reading under pressure was never going to be easy for her. Jim used to like to tell people he was a great driver who was stuck with a blind navigator. Retiring that line had also helped to preserve their marriage.

6

July 1 - Outside Calgary - around 8 a.m.

Jim walked up the stairs into the RV. Kelly was sitting at the dinette eating a pop tart and looking at her iPad mini. They had hit the jackpot at the Walmart a few days ago and bought ten boxes of the only pop tarts she would eat. They had also found that the Walmart stocked what they called Kelly-bread, Sara Lee Artesano, which was the only bread she would eat. They bought five loaves and a large Skippy Creamy Peanut Butter. Kelly would be able to eat for weeks.

Alex was still sleeping on the fold-out couch, her long, dark hair sprouting in all directions. She was making an odd little noise in her sleep, and he leaned in closer to get a look. Then he saw that she had her right hand up to her face and was sucking her thumb in her sleep. When was the last time she had done that? Not since she was a toddler. It was a disconcerting development, and Jim made a mental note to mention it to Joy later.

Jim could hear the water running in the shower, so that's what Joy was up to. He reached to his left and pressed the water button on the control panel to see how much they had left in the tank. He hadn't hooked up to the campground's water supply yet, so Joy was using the water they had on board. The system showed over one-third of a tank, so she should be fine if she doesn't stay in there too long. He turned off the water heater since she was unlikely to need more than the water that was already warm – it would also keep Joy from showering too long if the water suddenly turned cold.

He sat down across from Kelly. "Good morning, Kelly. I love you."

No response. She just kept staring at whatever was on her screen. Kelly was small for her age with fair skin (although not as fair as her mother) and light brown hair spilling down past her shoulders. In some ways she was more perceptive and focused than the average thirteen-year-old, in other ways she seemed less developed than her peers. She was on the autism spectrum which, for her, meant she often had trouble relating to other people and struggled in many social situations. She could become so overwhelmed by outside stimuli that she either shut down completely or lashed out.

In elementary school, she would get off the bus after school, walk in the house, go to her room, shut the door, and just stay there by herself for at least an hour to decompress after being around other people all day. She had noise-cancelling headphones in her desk at school that she was allowed to wear any time the classroom noise levels started to get to her, which meant she used them constantly.

After a brief stint at the public middle school that went horribly, Kelly switched to online school and her mental health had improved significantly. She still had good and bad days, but more of her days had been good. When she was having a really good day, there was nowhere else Jim wanted to be.

When she was happy, Kelly filled the room with joy and energy. She would become interested in something and her enthusiasm in discussing it would make everyone else interested in it as well. As a young child she went through a long period where she would pick a color for the day and everything she wore or played with had to be that color. It got to the point where Jim was sorting the fruit loops into separate containers by color so she would have the right breakfast for red day or yellow day. Joy had somehow helped her past that stage. She liked to have a routine – the family always kept a weekly calendar hanging on the wall in the kitchen so Kelly could know exactly what was going to happen every day that week, well ahead of time. They had been doing this since she was three and the scheduled items on the calendar were shown with pictures instead of words. Routine and predictability meant a lot to Kelly.

Jim knew the events of the last few weeks had done a number on Kelly's routine and she had been going back and forth from completely withdrawn in her own world to full-on meltdown with not much time spent between those two emotional levels. Lately, when she was mentally present, she had become physically clingy, especially to mom, and often talked in baby talk or animal sounds. For now, Jim decided to let her be. The family would find out soon enough where on the emotional spectrum she was going to land today, and whether she was going to moo or meow at them.

The shower door opened so Jim let Joy know he was back. "Hey Honey, I'm in here with the girls."

"Did you make any new friends?" This was a bit of a running joke between them as he tended to get into conversations with people in campgrounds. Occasionally that was a source of friction, especially if he was gone for long periods of time or neglected to plug in the RV on a hot day so the ladies were stuck without A/C while he chatted up a campground worker. Joy sometimes referred to him as chatty-Jim.

"I don't know if I'd call him a friend yet, but I did meet a guy at the campsite just across the road and I'll probably go hang out with him later if that's okay with you."

She laughed. "You know that we've met before, right? Whether I say it's okay or not, you're going to find a way to go chat some more. Just stick around while we get the girls up and dressed and figure out what else is on the schedule for today, then go hang out with your new friend. But you need to be back to help with lunch."

She came out of the bedroom now, dressed for a day hanging out inside the camper – cutoff shorts, a t-shirt, and Crocs. She had a pretty strict rule about no outside shoes in the living area of the camper and her Crocs were her inside shoes. Joy was in her early 40's and extremely fair skinned, in fact she had no pigment. Life with albinism and low vision hadn't been easy, but she was tough and very smart. She got a college degree in three years without ever seeing the whiteboards during the lectures or reading the printed textbooks. Every semester while she waited for her books to show up in audio format, she would either have to recruit other people to read them to her or use a magnifier to try to struggle her way through the materials – which nearly always resulted in a bad headache. Sometimes Jim had read chapters of her textbooks into a cassette recorder, but they both agreed that he was really bad at it, so it was only done in times of desperation.

Once when she could no longer handle the wait for a Stephen King short story to come out in audio format, she begged Jim to read it onto a cassette for her and was furious to find that Jim had inserted his own editorializations about every character's actions throughout the recording. That ended Jim's career reading books on tape. Although she and Jim occasionally jokingly referred to her as the evil albino, as people with albinism are often portrayed in movies and books, she was a good, dedicated mom who fiercely advocated for her kids with the school district, spoke out at school board meetings, and had become an expert at navigating the systems for her Deaf kid and her autistic kid. She used this knowledge to help other families of Deaf and hard of hearing children to maximize their children's potential as well. Her degree in psychology was being put to a severe test by the circumstances their children were going through.

"Kelly had pop tarts for breakfast and Alex is still out cold. Do you want me to get her moving? I should also hook us up to the water line and dump the tanks as long as were going to be here for a while." Jim was not very helpful with the emotional trauma the girls were working through, so he was anxious to make himself useful in other ways.

Joy squeezed past him (they were always squeezing past each other or bumping into one another in the tightly spaced camper, but it was all part of the camping experience) and sat down next to Kelly. "How are you this morning, honey?" She gave Kelly a little hug.

Kelly ignored her mom's question. "When is Alex getting up?"

"Dad's going to wake her up right now and get her bed put away. How about you climb up top and get dressed for the day."

This was part of the normal morning ritual, the sleeping bag and bedding that Alex used had to be packed away in the overhead storage and the fold-out couch returned to couch form to allow for a little bit more space inside the camper. While Kelly had her own little private sleeping area, Alex was stuck sleeping in the living room right next to the dining table. Alex was a good sport about it, though, and was the only member of the family who could sleep in that area without being disturbed by the rest of the family going through that area at night and in the morning. Again, Jim wished they had just one slide-out in the living/dining area to create a little bit more space and make the place seem more like a living area than a one-room camp house.

Jim bent down and gently shook Alex by the shoulder. As usual, she resisted and tried to roll over rather than open her eyes. At least she pulled her thumb out of her mouth. Jim persisted until she finally opened her eyes and gave him a look that screamed leave me alone. Jim pointed at his wrist and signed, "Time to wake up." When she glowered back at him, he made a stern face and signed, "Now." That always seemed to work. Alex was a sweet, good-natured kid who couldn't stay mad at anyone for long, especially not her dad.

Jim was always amazed that someone who had been dealt the hand Alex got in life – Deaf, cerebral palsy, multiple major surgeries to literally every part of her body from head to toes – could be the most empathetic, most loving person he'd ever met. He hoped she wasn't going to lose that beautiful attitude because of what they had gone through over the last few weeks.

"Okay, okay, I'm going," she said this at the higher-than-normal volume that she used at times when she was completely Deaf. Alex had cochlear implants that allowed her to hear when she wore the external hardware, but right now those units were in their drying case where they spent every night so they would be ready for the next day. She dutifully maintained the hardware and made sure to recharge the batteries every night. She was very responsible for a thirteen-year-old when it came to the $20,000 worth of equipment that she wore hanging from her ears every day. Alex had her first implant surgery when she was three and it took about six months before she could be trusted to keep the external hardware on her head without trying to yank it off. Once she got used to the stimulation in her head and internalized that it was helping her to hear the sounds around her, she became more cooperative.

After having a second surgery so that she would have implants on both sides, she had been great about using the technology almost all the time. She still needed a sign language interpreter to help her follow the lessons at school where the chaos of the classroom reduced the effectiveness of her devices, but at home she was usually able to keep up with conversations. Through years and years of practice and speech therapy, her vocabulary was way above grade level and most of her words were pronounced correctly. In her early elementary school days, she would occasionally get up on a Saturday and tell Jim, "I Deaf today," but she hadn't had a Deaf day in a long time until the last few weeks.

During their recent travels across Western Canada, she would take off both of her external devices without telling anyone and just be Deaf until someone else noticed. When she was little, her behavior when she was Deaf was much worse than when she could hear. Back then, she was talented at looking away when she knew mom or dad were signing something they wanted her to do. Jim hadn't noticed any difference in her behavior, between Deaf time and hearing time, during their travels in the RV together this summer.

Alex got up and she and Joy had a brief conversation that Jim didn't follow because he only saw it out of the corner of his eye, and he was not as skilled in ASL as them. Then she headed to the bedroom to get dressed. When she was gone, Jim quickly packed up the bedding and folded up the couch. Now the place was ready for the next twelve hours or so until it would be time to start the whole bedtime ritual all over again.

Jim looked around and noticed that Joy was staring at him. "What? Did I do something wrong?"

She shook her head and then very slowly signed, "We need to talk outside later." He nodded that he understood.

They hadn't had much chance to talk privately about the issues the girls were dealing with since they were all packed in tight quarters, had been moving around a lot, and Kelly might or might not be following everything that was said within the camper. He looked around to make sure Alex was still in the bedroom and the curtain to the over the cab sleeping area that had become Kelly's little private space was still pulled shut. Then he moved in close to Joy, and signed, "After breakfast, screen time." If there was one thing that was sure to keep the girls occupied, it was screen time.

Then he said, "Want some breakfast? I'm cooking as long as it's bagels in the toaster."

7

June 6 - Duluth - around 1 a.m.

Jim was a little bit perturbed that they were experiencing a power outage on a summer night when the weather was perfect. He was used to having the power go out during heavy snowstorms and even the occasional thunderstorm. A few summers back, when the city was doing work on the main road a block away, the power went out multiple times every day for weeks, but that was during the day. He reached over and picked up his phone – 1:04 a.m. – he had only been in bed for a couple hours.

On the off chance that it was an internal problem, he got up, carefully made his way down the hall to the living room and looked out the window. Nope, the streetlight across the way was out, so this was more than just his house. He thought about going on the Minnesota Power website to report the outage but decided that could wait until morning. *Somebody else is probably calling it in right now anyway and their computers have probably already detected it.* Using the flashlight on his phone he went back down the hall and dug around in the hall closet until he found a couple of battery-powered lanterns they sometimes used in the camper. He turned them on to see if they still worked. One of them worked fine and the other was a bit weak. He went to the kitchen and found replacement batteries for the weak one then put one lantern in each of the girls' bedrooms so if they woke up during the night they wouldn't be stuck in the dark.

Rather than risking waking Joy up by getting back in the bed, he went back to the living room and set himself up on the couch. The decorative pillows Joy insisted they needed to have on the couch seemed comfortable enough. Jim was fast asleep in less than two minutes.

8

December 16th - 4 years earlier - Duluth

"I kind of liked the last one better. Which model was it?" Jim and Joy are sitting on the couch in the RV they will eventually purchase, looking at a flyer of the different floorplans the local RV dealer has in their indoor showroom. They have narrowed their decision down to a Four Winds class C motorhome, but Joy wasn't yet committed to which one they would be driving home that day.

They were planning a trip to Alaska for the coming summer, but didn't have confidence that the twenty-year-old, used motorhome they've had for the last few years is up to the challenge. In four years, and six big road trips, their RV has broken down twice. Both breakdowns were stressful experiences that they would like to avoid repeating. It's over 3,000 miles from Duluth to Denali, with long stretches through remote areas, and neither of them want to be stranded on the Alaska Highway.

"The one we're sitting in is the 28A, it's three feet shorter than the one we have now, but the floorplan is really similar, other than the split bathroom and shower." Jim is pointing to the flyer where Joy has drawn big red X's through the models that are not in stock and has written the prices and her own little descriptions next to the floorplans for the rest of the models. For some reason she has written "Cheepy" next to the 28A. While the price was less than the other models they had looked at, it didn't seem that cheap to Jim. "The last one was the 31WV. It's longer and has a slide, and you liked the big closet across from the bathroom. But it's quite a bit more money." Joy's description next to the floorplan for the 31WV says "Dreamy."

"Right, well I didn't like the one where the bed folded up when the slide was in. I want to put that nicer mattress on the bed and that won't work." She put another big red X on the page. Pointing at the page she said, "This one doesn't have a sofa, so where would Alex sleep? Plus, it's even more expensive. How can it be more expensive when it's smaller and has less furniture?" Another red X.

Through the process of elimination, they eventually work their way down to one floorplan left on the page without a red X, the 28A.

Jim jumps up from the couch. "I'm going to go find Joe and tell him what we want before you change your mind."

They sign all the paperwork and drive their brand new RV home to show the girls. It's the biggest, most expensive family Christmas present they will ever receive. Joy likes to name their vehicles, so she asks the girls for suggestions. Alex looks at the Four Winds stickers on the side of the RV and dubs their new ride "Windy." With no objections, the name sticks.

9

∽

July 1 - Outside Calgary - morning

Joy, Jim, and Alex had bagels with cream cheese for breakfast while Kelly stayed in her private clubhouse up top. Once she knew there was going to be screen time, possibly a Disney movie, Alex was agreeable to starting the day being able to hear. Most of the DVDs in their collection had captions, but Alex still enjoyed the movie experience more when she could hear.

After breakfast Jim decided to go outside to hook up the water hose and dump the waste tanks. As he was headed towards the door Joy stopped him. "You're not going to wear that shirt all day, are you? You wore it to bed last night."

Jim had completely forgotten about the Minnesota Wild shirt. "Pretty perceptive for a blind woman. I think I'll keep it on while I do the dirty work outside and change it afterwards."

"Don't you dare try to wear that in the bed again tonight." In addition to her rule about outside shoes in the living area, Joy also had a strict rule about outside clothes on her bed. "That shirt better go straight into the dirty laundry when you come back in."

"I think this shirt is going to be retired from service until the Wild play their next game, if they ever play another game." With that Jim stepped out to finish with the hookups.

Walking around to the back of the camper, Jim admired how much privacy each of the campsites had at this campground. So many RV parks maximized their occupancy by leaving just enough space between sites for the utility box, the water hookup, and sometimes a fire pit or a picnic table. This place left plenty of unused space between the sites and left the trees and other foliage in that space so Jim couldn't even see the campers on either side of them. He could hear some kids playing somewhere off in the distance, but it felt almost secluded behind the camper.

Jim was an old pro now at the process of using the utilities at a campground. First, he found the campground water spigot and tested it to make sure it was working properly. Once he was confident the water was working right, he opened up the rear storage compartment where his water hose was hanging coiled from a hook, took out the hose, and attached one end to the spigot and the other end to the receptacle on the camper. Since their water tank was low, he left the switch on the tank fill setting and turned the water back on.

It would take about five minutes for the tank to fill, so he pulled on his dumping gloves and pulled out the storage tote where he kept the dirty waste hose. The tote was tightly wrapped in gray duct tape to hold it together from the recent damage, and Jim thought about the many colors of duct tape he had put to use over the years, especially in the last few weeks. After pulling the lid off the tote, he pulled out the hose and extended it.

Once it was extended, he inspected the brown duct tape he had wrapped around the holes in the hose from the 6th. The tape closely matched the color of the hose and seemed to be holding up pretty well. It wasn't pretty, but it was a waste hose, and he wasn't ready to spend money on a new one when a little duct tape could keep this one operational. No need to put fresh tape on yet. He hooked up one end of the hose to the RV dump pipe and stuck the other end into the campground sewer receptacle. He pulled the lever to let out the contents of the black water tank first and waited for all the contents to empty out, then he pushed the lever for the black water tank back in and pulled the lever for the gray water tank so that tank could empty out.

It had been a few days since they dumped and it took a while for both tanks to empty. Normally after Jim dumped the tanks, he would pack everything back up because the family would be heading to their next location. He had to stop and remind himself they would be here for at least one more night and he could just leave the hose until tomorrow. He went back to the water intake and flipped the switch from tank fill to city water, packed his storage tote and gloves back in the storage compartment and headed back into the RV with a mischievous grin on his face.

As Jim opened the door and stepped into the camper he began to sing, "Oh Canada, our home and native land...." Jim had a horrible singing voice, but the one concession the family made to him was that he could sing "Oh Canada" as much as he wanted on Canada Day. This tradition started on their trip to Alaska a few years back when they were coming back through Canada on July 1st. As someone who had played youth hockey and gone to Canada for hockey camps, Jim knew all the words, although he sang them poorly.

The singing got its intended results. Joy groaned, Alex reached up to the sides of her head like she needed to yank off her listening technology to save herself, and Kelly gave a big smile and ran over to hug Jim while he sang. As soon as the song reached its conclusion, Joy called for a group hug to celebrate the end of the torture.

"I guess you want me to go hang out with my new friend the rest of the day now, huh?" Jim joked. "I probably have at least ten encores in me before my voice gives out."

"Your voice gave out before I met you. You need to change that stinky shirt and then the girls are going to watch a movie while we relax outside before the sun gets too high."

10

June 6 - Duluth - around 2 a.m.

Jim's sleep was short-lived. What sounded like multiple police cars with sirens blaring jolted him awake again. He grabbed his phone from the coffee table and checked the time – 1:53 a.m.

Less than a minute later the thought of getting more sleep left him when he heard gunfire coming from the main road a block away to the east – the same place the sound of the sirens had come from. He froze for just a moment, then sprang into action. His kids' bedrooms were at the front of the house and their windows faced in the direction of whatever was going on out there. He hurried down the hall to Kelly's room and tried to wake her up gently.

"Hey, sweetie, the power went out. How about you go join mom in our bed, so she doesn't get scared. I need to fix something and mom will be all alone."

Kelly was very sleepy, not fully awake. She had no interest in getting out of bed or even responding to her dad.

"Okay, honey, I'm going to carry you to mom, alright? You just keep your eyes closed. Here's your Pinkie Bear, can you hold onto him?"

Jim put one arm under her upper back and one arm under her thighs and tried to lift her up. Nope. That wasn't going to work. Did he get old and weak, or had she just grown too much?

"Okay, honey, I really need you to help me out right now. Your mom needs you." Right then he heard what sounded like a couple bursts of automatic weapons fire, maybe a little further away but he couldn't be sure. The urgency of his task ramped up.

Jim pulled Kelly up into a sitting position, then grabbed her in a big hug and lifted her up. She put one arm around his neck and held tightly to her stuffed bear with the other arm. He was just able to keep her feet above the floor and work his way across the hall to the master bedroom. He wasn't able to set her down gently in the bed, she went down heavily, and the jolt woke Joy up.

"What are you doing?" Joy asked, still half asleep.

"I can't explain right now, but the girls need to spend the rest of the night in here with you. I'm going to get Alex."

"No Jim. I won't get any sleep with the girls in here. Alex is a sleep ninja. She'll be kicking me all night."

Quietly, but sternly, Jim said, "This is important. I'll explain when I get back here with Alex, but I have to hurry. Don't let Kelly leave this room."

With that he rushed across the hall.

Alex was going to be trickier; she was a heavy sleeper and there was no way he was going to carry her against her will. She had a way of turning her body into a noodle when she didn't want to be moved. It was like she literally turned every muscle in her body into mush, so lifting her was like trying to lift eighty pounds of Jell-O. He had never seen anything like it before. If anyone ever wanted to kidnap her, they would need two strong guys and a wheelbarrow to move her.

Jim shook her gently, then harder, then rolled her onto her back, all with no effect at waking her up. He grabbed her arms and pulled her up into a sitting position. That got her eyes open. He signed, "You need to sleep with mom." That got a tired, quizzical look. He signed, "Hurry, please." That got a tired stare. Finally, he bent down and tried to lift her up. He was not successful, but it got a reaction.

"Fine, I'm going." Somehow it was both a sleepy voice and a yell. She slowly got out of the bed and started walking toward the door. She turned to look back at him. "Why is Kelly's lantern here?" He hadn't even realized that the girls each had their own specific lantern and he had put them in the wrong bedrooms.

He signed, "Plug, all done."

She furrowed her brow, "Oh, the power is out."

He signed, "Yes."

Joy got out of the bed to let Alex in. She was awake now and wanted an explanation. She put one of the lanterns on the bedside table and Jim could see the girls already seemed to be asleep again.

Jim and Joy went out into the hall and shut the bedroom door. The light from the lantern in Kelly's room was providing enough of a glow in the hallway to see each other. Jim made sure they didn't stand in the doorway of either of the girls' bedrooms. He wanted a solid wall on their east flank just in case.

Jim started, "The power is out. I heard sirens out on the avenue followed by lots of shooting." Just then there was what sounded like an explosion further off in the distance to the Northeast. *Was that the gas station by the highway?* "The girls' windows face that way so I wanted to put them in our room so they have an extra wall between them and any stray bullets."

She now understood the gravity of the situation. "Will that wall stop a bullet?"

Jim shrugged as he said, "I don't know, but it's better to have two walls of protection than just one wall or a window."

"What are we going to do?" She was clearly scared now, for the safety of all of them.

"I'm going to grab a gun and stand watch the rest of the night. The doors are locked and I'll be up listening for anything coming near us. You go stay with the girls and keep them in our room. If we need to, we can all go in the basement. Hopefully the police will have whatever is going on under control quickly."

She gave him a hug, "I'm not going to be able to sleep again tonight."

He nodded. "Yeah, but you can stay close to the girls and calm them down when they wake up in the wrong bed. Don't know if either of them will remember changing beds during the night. Keep them in our room and try not to let them see how stressed you are. I love you."

They hugged a little bit longer, then she went into the bedroom and closed the door behind her. Using his phone as a flashlight, Jim went down the stairs to the basement and opened the safe where he kept his guns. He was not a hunter or a gun enthusiast. He owned two handguns that hadn't been out of the safe in a long time. One was a six-shot revolver and the other was a 9mm that loaded through a clip that held ten rounds.

He knew how to safely handle both weapons and to shoot them, but he couldn't have spoken intelligently about them, nor did he care to. He got the revolver many years ago after a break-in at the apartment he was living in during college. The 9mm was purchased soon after they moved into their current house when they were the only house on their cul-de-sac and felt isolated and alone at night. Jim had also purchased a security system back then. Now all the lots in their neighborhood were filled with houses and he didn't feel isolated at all. He moved the safe down to the basement and forgotten all about those nights lying awake wondering if the noise he just heard was Duluth's version of the BTK murderer trying to gain access to his family.

The safe had twelve bullets that worked in the revolver sitting in a box next to the gun and twenty bullets for the 9mm already loaded into two clips. He silently prayed to not have to use either gun, then grabbed the 9mm and its two full clips of ammunition. Weapon in hand, he headed back upstairs to sit and listen, but set the gun and the clips next to each other on the coffee table. Jim was only going to load the weapon if he needed to.

In the living room, he checked the time on his phone again. It was 2:08. *What time is sunrise in early June?* He tried to think back to his days delivering the morning newspaper and thought that in the summer it was usually getting fairly light by the time he finished his paper route at 5:30. That meant he maybe he had three more hours until sunrise. Those were going to be three long hours.

11

∾

July 1 - Outside Calgary - after breakfast

Jim swung the TV out from the wall and turned it on. Joy helped the girls find a DVD that they could both agree to watch – this took a while, and they almost went through their whole collection of DVDs before consensus was reached. They eventually decided on an old Muppets movie.

Once the show started, Joy grabbed her sunglasses and Jim and Joy slipped outside. They stepped around to the back of the camper where there was still some shade at this time of the morning. Jim pulled a couple of camp chairs out of the rear storage compartment, and they sat down close to each other.

Joy started the conversation. "They both need to start therapy and it can't wait. I know we said we would treat this like a long vacation, but they know it's not a vacation and they're dealing with PTSD. They need help from an expert who knows how to work with kids that have been through traumatic experiences. We need to get them started now. I don't have the right training and I'm too close to them to be able to give them the help they need."

Jim sighed, "I know. I want them to get help as much as you do. Alex was sucking her thumb in her sleep this morning like a baby. Last night Kelly tried to communicate with me in meows and woofs. They're both regressing into toddlers. But we've been living in Walmart parking lots and cheap campgrounds to save money. We're probably only going to find that type of expertise in a bigger city where it's tough to get around in a motorhome. Nobody here is going to take our health insurance, if our health insurance even exists anymore. We don't know anything about how the health care system works up here." He paused for a couple seconds to calm himself. "Look, I can try to do some research later today. Maybe I'll get lucky and find a place in Calgary that specializes in PTSD for kids with special needs. Even if I do, we're probably going to have to pay as we go, and we aren't bringing in any money right now."

Joy had always been conscious of their money situation. She was a saver who hated being in debt. They had paid off their previous house in six years and when they sold that house and bought the house they owned now, her goal was to pay off that mortgage in five years – a goal that they achieved. She hated paying interest to the bank. Years back, she had unilaterally removed Jim from the monthly bill paying responsibility after he paid one bill late and they were charged a $25 late payment fee. He only got the responsibility back when she was pregnant with the girls. She took their current financial situation very seriously, but helping her kids to heal was her number one priority right now.

"We both have college educations. We can probably find some paying work wherever we find a good psychologist. Even if we just work for cash or for low wages, at least we might be able to bring in enough to pay for the therapy. We have to do something to get them the help they need."

Jim shook his head. "I'm not sure if it would even be legal for us to work for cash or to work at all without a work visa. I think we would need to apply for amnesty or work visas to be able to get jobs, maybe we need to apply for refugee status in the country. At least that's how I think it works in the U.S. We don't want to get in trouble and get deported when we don't know what the situation is in Minnesota. And we can't go to Canadian jail and leave our kids to be sent to some Canadian foster home. How about I add applying for a work visa and applying for amnesty to my research list? I really wish that satellite internet was still working. Have you tried the campground Wi-Fi yet?"

She slowly shook her head. "It's not good. The network shows up as an option, but even at 7:30 this morning I couldn't get anything to work using it. Maybe it would work if you went and sat right by the office."

He nodded. "Why is it so hard to find a campground that has decent Wi-Fi? I'll take my iPad over by the office and see if it works there later." He held up his phone. "This Canadian cell phone only has one bar showing right now, so it's probably going to be slow trying to do research from our campsite. If my laptop and our satellite dish had survived the trip, researching would be much more efficient."

Just then, Joy started sobbing. She had been strong for the girls now for the last three plus weeks and all of those built-up emotions were spilling out. "What are we going to do about school this fall? Where are we going to live when winter comes? I haven't spoken to my mom since before we left. What if she's dead and I wasn't there for her?" Tears were flowing freely now, but she kept going. "We had a house, jobs, family, friends. We had money saved for college and retirement. We were doing good with the Little Free Libraries and the Lions Club. We were doing everything right and now it's all gone. We live like nomads in a fucking camper in a foreign country. Our kids are traumatized. I'm traumatized. What do we do when the money runs out? Who's going to help us? How could this have happened in America?"

Jim crouched in front of Joy and held her tightly. She was sobbing uncontrollably.

"Hey, it's going to be okay. We are all okay. We have each other and we are smart and tough and we're a great team. Lots of countries have gone through unrest and come out the other side. We don't know anything right now. It could be that things will calm down and we can go back and pick things back up sort of where we left off. Our house is probably fine. Our 401k balances have probably taken a beating, but they could recover. The treasury bonds and CDs we had will probably still be there when everything settles down. Maybe by September we're back in our house and America has regained its sanity." He took a few seconds to think.

"Look, worst case scenario is we apply for amnesty or work visas and get jobs here for as long as it takes for America to become America again. We get the kids into therapy, enroll them in school up here, and find an apartment to rent to get us through the winter. Eventually we are going to find out what is happening in the U.S. There has to be information getting out, we just haven't figured out how to find it yet."

They held each other for a long time, Joy getting all of her sadness and fears out. She needed this emotional release now so she could go back to being strong and confident around the girls.

As the sun rose higher, they lost the shade they were sitting in. That was a sign that Joy needed to get back inside so she wouldn't burn. Joy wiped her face and got herself as presentable as she could. With the movie going, the girls would be unlikely to notice she had been crying. They walked back to the camper door, arms around each other. They were a team and Jim was determined to make sure their team supported each other. Their team was going to win no matter what the world threw at them. He wasn't sure what winning would look like, but he was sure they had what it took to do it, if they worked together.

12

February 13th - 13 years earlier - evening

"Bring that wheelchair over and help me get into it." Joy was in a hospital bed, hooked up to an IV, and her words were a little slow coming out.

Jim gave her a wary look. "Honey, you just had a C-Section a few hours ago. The doctors said you shouldn't get out of bed at all tonight."

"I need to see my girls." Her voice was stronger now.

Jim understood why she felt such a strong need to see the girls tonight. Their daughters had been born that afternoon at 28 weeks gestation after Joy had spent a month in the hospital while the doctors and nurses tried desperately to keep their babies in her womb. Their daughters' survival was not a certainty. The girls were each just over two and a half pounds, with lungs not yet fully developed. Jim wanted Joy to see the girls tonight just as badly as Joy did. Their babies were in incubators in the NICU and would not be able to travel down the hall to visit their mom. If Joy was going to see them tonight, Jim was going to have to sneak her out of her room and across the hospital.

Jim had been able to go directly from the operating room to the NICU with the girls, and had been there all afternoon as the doctors and nurses hooked them up to ventilators, monitors and IVs. He called Pastor Tim and received instructions on how to baptize the girls himself – just in case. He wasn't one hundred percent confident he had the power to sanctify the sterilized water he used for the ritual, but they weren't getting a Lutheran minister into the NICU that day, and he wasn't taking any chances that his kids would miss the path to salvation. If Jim could help Joy to see their daughters alive before God took one, or both of them, he needed to do it.

Jim pulled the wheelchair next to the bed and locked the wheels into place. "Okay. You need to use every muscle you can to help me get you in this chair. We really don't want to have to pick you up off the floor. I don't want to get kicked out of the hospital on the day our kids are born."

Working together, they get Joy transferred from the bed to the chair. Jim makes sure none of the tubes from the IV are tangled on anything and he pulls the IV stand out from behind the bed. He buckles the seat-belt on the chair, so Joy doesn't slip out the bottom if she drifts back to sleep, and they carefully make their way out of the room. Jim thinks they must be quite a sight as he pushes the wheelchair with one hand while pulling the IV stand with his other hand. It's slow going, but nobody tries to stop them, and they make it to the NICU without incident.

The inside of the NICU is a maze of incubators, cribs, monitors, beeping noises, and flashing lights. It can be disorienting to a first-time visitor, especially if a bunch of alarms are going off. Jim has spent hours here already and has the workings of the place figured out, but to Joy it is surprising, and not what she expected. "Where are the girls?" She asks in a whispered tone.

"Almost there." Jim is pushing much more slowly now, not wanting to go off course and bump into anything important. Joy has taken hold of the IV stand so Jim can better steer the wheelchair.

A nurse sees Jim struggling and comes over to help. "We were not expecting to see you tonight, mom. I think you're supposed to be in bed until tomorrow afternoon." The nurse gives Joy a wink as she says this.

Then she helps Jim maneuver the wheelchair into the space between the two incubators holding their daughters.

The nurse shows Joy how to open the little door to the incubator while Jim gives her some hand sanitizer. Once her hands are dry, she opens the door to Kelly's little space and reaches in to touch her first-born daughter for the first time. "I love you so much my baby girl. I'm going to be here for you every day. I can't wait to hold you and hug you."

Joy just touched Kelly for a long time, tears streaming down her face. Then she turned to Jim. "I need to see Alex. Can you help me turn around?"

Joy spent an equal amount of time with Alex. All she could do at this point was touch her babies through a small opening in a big plastic bubble, but she was going to do it until she couldn't keep her eyes open.

Jim felt better about sneaking Joy out of her bed against her doctor's orders. The nurses seemed fine with it, and they were now partners in crime. He wasn't sure how Joy was able to sit up this long after having her guts cut open a few hours ago, but she gave no indication that the pain was going to force her back to bed. He knew the next days and weeks were going to be full of ups and downs, but tonight he started to understand just how dedicated a mom Joy was going to be.

13

∾

June 6 - Duluth - around 2:15 a.m.

The house was silent. Jim grabbed the lantern out of Kelly's room and put it in the dining room just around the corner from the living room. He wanted enough light so that he wasn't sitting in complete darkness, but not so much that the light could be seen through the curtains to anyone outside. No need to bring any attention to his house from anyone who was doing the shooting outside.

He sat down on the floor below window level and picked up his phone thinking he had lots of time to report the power outage now. When he opened the Safari app, he got a message that he had no internet connection. *That's strange, the cell service is usually only one or two bars here at the house, but it's enough to get to a website even when the Wi-Fi is out.* He looked at the top of his phone and it said no service. "That's ominous," he said aloud.

Jim sat thinking for a few minutes. He wondered if the Wi-Fi was out at the source and if he could get internet if he plugged the router into another power source. That got him wishing he had done more than just consider putting solar panels on the roof. He liked the idea, but his electric bills were still pretty reasonable, and it seemed like the long payback period on a project like that made it less urgent. Occasional, brief power outages were just part of life in Northern Minnesota and the power always came back on before the food spoiled or the house froze. Jim hadn't factored a scenario of sitting in the dark wishing his internet router was working while a small-scale war was waged just a couple blocks away into his calculations. For now, he decided to just wait on the power coming back on.

Okay. I'm sitting on the floor in the dark with no internet and probably three hours until it's light outside. How am I going to pass the time?

He started scrolling through pictures on his phone, reminding himself of all of their family trips and the experiences they had together. Vacation pictures had always been a great way for Jim to get to a happy place.

He found some pictures from their first trip to Arches National Park. They had arrived in the late afternoon, but wanted to at least see something before heading to the campground, so they took the short side road that led to Delicate Arch. The parking lot was a long ways from the arch, but there was a trail that allowed visitors to get closer. Only Jim and Kelly were interested in taking the trail. Joy and Alex went back to the camper. The trail didn't actually get them all that close to the arch, but it was a fun little hike.

On their way back it started to rain. It didn't feel like a heavy rain to Jim, and they got back to the RV just a little bit damp. Jim started driving them back towards the main road, but had to stop because there were cars backed up and what looked like a huge river flowing across the road up ahead. The river had to be about 100 feet wide and was carrying debris across the road and further downhill. Other people were out of their vehicles watching all of the water and debris as it flowed past. Some were wondering if they were going to be trapped for hours. Eventually a park ranger came from the other side of the water in a big truck and drove across the river. He told them anyone with a heavy vehicle would be fine, just go slowly, so the girls buckled up and Jim drove the RV around the line of cars and through the water. When they came out on the other side, Jim declared, "We made it." And Kelly added, "And we lived!"

Jim smiled looking at the pictures of the girls standing in the road in front of the flowing water. They were so excited for some reason. That was the highlight of that trip for them up to that point. They looked so young in those pictures. They were eight at the time. When they came back to the park the next day, Kelly had charged up every rock formation they came upon. She just loved to climb. Sometimes Jim couldn't keep up with her and she would get to a scary height before he could get there and hold onto her. Even after all the parks they had visited over the years, Arches was still her favorite. Any place that had rocks to climb was a great place in Kelly's world.

He scrolled back a little further and found some photos taken at Great Sand Dunes National Park. Those pictures made Jim laugh out loud. They hadn't planned on visiting that park, hadn't even known it existed until the night before. They had been at a campground somewhere in Southwest Colorado and were planning to go to Mesa Verde National Park the next day. When he was mapping their drive for the next day, he saw that they were only thirty minutes away from the Sand Dunes and decided they should at least see what it was. They got to the park around 8 a.m. and all piled out of the camper. The first photo was of Joy and the girls with the dunes in the background. The expressions on the girls' faces in the picture were priceless. All three of them were being swarmed by mosquitoes and only Joy could hold a pose for a picture face. The girls were swatting and cringing. Immediately after the picture the girls sprinted back to the camper and wouldn't come back out. Jim wandered around taking photos of the dunes for about thirty minutes and that was the end of the Great Sand Dunes for his family.

He scrolled back a little bit further and found the photos of the first time he used duct tape for RV repair – it wouldn't be the last time. The weather stripping on the over the cab sleeping area on their old, used RV had dried out and outlived its usefulness. Somewhere along the highway in Southwest Colorado it started working its way loose and by the time they got to their campground, five feet of it was flapping loose in the breeze. Jim had grabbed a roll of white duct tape and climbed up on the roof of the RV. A couple of neighboring campers came by with a ladder and with Jim at the top, a helpful neighbor at the bottom, and a push broom to reach the middle area that was too far away from either of them, they were able to push the weather stripping back into the slot where it was supposed to stay. Then they used the tape to run a number of long strips the entire length from the roof to just above the cab. Jim would start each strip at the top and work it as far as he could without falling off the roof, then toss the roll to the helper who secured it at the bottom. They used the broom to push down the tape in the areas they couldn't reach. When they were done you had to look closely to tell that the weather stripping was actually white duct tape done hastily in a campground. That tape held tight through a lot of miles and all kinds of weather. It was still on the RV when Jim and Joy traded it in for their new motorhome.

Jim thought of all the people he had met on the road who had offered a helping hand when his family needed one and the times when he helped out a fellow traveler. That weather stripping would have been impossible for Jim to fix by himself without a ladder, but, like magic, a couple of other campers just showed up, with a ladder, ready to help. The day their fan belt broke on a two-lane highway in the middle of nowhere Utah, and a guy stopped to check on them. He not only knew how to replace the belt, but actually had an extra one just the right size for their V-8 Ford engine. The two old guys in Nova Scotia who noticed that the cargo carrier Jim had on the back of the camper was about to fall off and got his attention, then found a bolt in their trunk the right size to replace the bolt that had broken. The guy at the Chevy dealership in Hinton, Alberta who welded the heat plate back onto the exhaust pipe after it came loose and then refused to charge Jim for the work because it only took a couple minutes and wasn't worth the paperwork. There were so many good people everywhere and traveling around had given Jim the opportunity to meet some of those good people.

He checked the time – 3:45 – getting closer to sunrise. Still no power. At least he hadn't heard any more shots or explosions.

14

July 1 - Outside Calgary - late morning

While the girls continued to watch the movie, Jim went to work in the kitchen area mixing up flour, eggs, water, milk, and butter into a batter then putting the batter into the fridge to settle for a while.

After the movie ended, Jim announced he would be making his world-famous crepes for lunch (they were only world famous to the four people in the camper, but that was part of Jim's schtick). Normally they didn't do crepes on the road, but Jim thought it would be a special way to celebrate Canada Day so he bought all the kitchen supplies and ingredients he would need a few days ago at Walmart. Kelly was particularly excited as crepes had become her favorite meal. Whether it counted as a meal or a dessert was an argument that could be had. She piled her crepe with chocolate chips and a sprinkle of sugar before eating it in a gooey mess. Alex preferred to sprinkle cinnamon and sugar on her crepe – which also seemed to Jim more like dessert than a meal. Joy was a Nutella crepe gal, which also seemed like a dessert topping to Jim.

At Walmart, Jim found a pan that was very similar to the pan he used at home, so he was confident that he could cook the crepes, if he could get the heat level on the burner right on the stove in the camper.

In four years traveling in this camper they had never once used the stove-top for cooking. When you're always on the go, you don't have time to stop and cook meals. In fact, when they had packed the RV for their three week trip to Alaska, they used the oven as an extra storage area rather than for cooking. Joy had stuffed two-liter bottles of apple juice and eight-packs of drink boxes into the oven until the door could barely shut. It had served them well as a convenient extra cupboard on that trip, but now he was going to find out if the stove actually worked.

Jim figured out how to spark the burner and got it going. He warmed up the pan, then buttered it up and poured in enough batter for the first crepe – Kelly always got the first crepe, so she was crowded in right next to him watching the process closely and holding her plate.

"MMMM, crepe," she said excitedly. Bouncing up and down on her toes.

"Okay, honey. I'm going to need to you back up a bit so I can flip your crepe. We don't have as much room here as in the kitchen at home. Can you stand by the fridge for thirty seconds?"

She danced away a few feet, still clearly excited and watching closely while Jim lifted the pan, swirled the now solid crepe around a little and did his magic crepe flip with a flick of the wrist. The crepe slid out of the pan, flipped halfway over and Jim caught it back in the pan so he could cook the other side.

This got an "OOOHHH" from Kelly who knew her chocolatey mess was almost ready. She did a little twirl while holding her plate above her head.

A minute later Jim was sliding the crepe carefully onto Kelly's plate. With a big smile she scampered to the dinette and sat down at her regular spot - a bowl of chocolate chips and a shaker filled with sugar were on the table ready for her. She started piling the chocolate chips onto the crepe.

"Okay, Alex, yours is next." Jim was greasing up the pan for the second crepe.

"Mom can have the next one if she's hungry." This was the usual routine. Alex was always so gracious and wanted everyone else in the family to be happy. She was always willing to put herself last if someone else wanted to go first. Jim and Joy sometimes called her their little Switzerland, because she didn't want to take sides and offend anyone.

"Nope, this one has your name on it, unless I mess it up and it turns into a disaster. In that case it would be mom's." He was pouring the batter and swirling it around to thin it out and cover the bottom of the pan.

"If you make a messy crepe pile, we'll save that one for you dad." Joy needled him.

With a mouthful of chocolate, Kelly declared. "If you don't want it, I'll eat it."

Jim made six crepes in all. Kelly and Joy each had two. Alex and Jim each had one. There was enough batter left over to make another four or five at another meal, so Jim packed it away in the fridge.

The movie and the crepe lunch felt like normal times. Like a Saturday at home, but with less space in the kitchen and dining room. They all had a great meal together. It was wonderful.

15

June 1 - Duluth - late morning

Jim always got a little bit jazzed up weeks before their annual summer trip. Even though this year's scheduled trip was still a few weeks away, he decided to do the annual de-winterizing of the camper and making sure everything was ready to roll when the time came.

De-winterizing wasn't a big deal. In the fall, Jim drained all the water out of the camper and put some antifreeze into the tanks and water lines. In the spring, Jim needed to get that antifreeze out of the tanks and lines, put the drain cap back on the water heater, and fill up the water tank. He also had to turn a few switches within the bowels of the RV that controlled the flow of the water. In the fall the switches went one way, in the spring he turned them back the other way. His first year with this camper the switches were a Rubik's Cube like problem for Jim. He tried them every different way but couldn't get hot water no matter what he did. Eventually he had to bring the RV to the shop and have a service technician show him how the switches should go. He immediately took photos of the switches and saved those photos in his favorites. Now he just pulled up the photos in the fall and the spring when he was performing his semi-annual service.

Jim was very careful about the process – making sure he didn't get any antifreeze into the water heater and ensuring he got all of the antifreeze out of the water lines. They didn't drink the water out of the tanks – just a family rule – but Joy wouldn't appreciate getting antifreeze in the face during her first RV shower of the year. He filled up the water tank about one-third of the way with water while leaving the switches so they by-passed the water heater. Then he turned on the water pump and opened every water valve, hot and cold, in the bathroom, shower, and kitchen until all the water and antifreeze ran out of the system.

Once the system was dry, he turned off the water pump, shut all the valves, turned the switches to their spring position, put the cap on the water heater, and filled the water tank back up to a little over the halfway point. Half a tank of water was a lot of weight to carry on the road, but he intended to spend at least their first night or two on the road off the grid so they would need the water for showers and flushing the toilet.

He checked the level of the propane tank. It was at about seventy-five percent full, which was about the upper limit of what the tank was allowed to hold. He had forgotten to check to see if the RV shop had topped it off a couple weeks back, so he was glad to see that they had.

After unhooking his water hose and packing it away, he walked around the RV to make sure none of the compartments were open and nothing was out of place, then he hopped in and drove to the gas station. The gas tank was more than half full already, but Jim had learned that having a full tank when they left for vacation allowed them to keep their momentum on that first morning. He pumped in about twenty-five gal-lons then pulled up to the RV dump station that the gas station let you use if you bought gas.

He did his usual RV dump routine in about five minutes and was on his way back home with a fully gassed up, halfway water-filled, and com-pletely waste-emptied RV. He would probably do some cleaning over the next couple weekends, but all they needed to do was load up their food, clothes, bedding, and electronics and they would be ready to roll. Jim wasn't quite there yet, but in another couple weeks, he would be in the grips of vacation fever, that time where every free minute was dedicated to planning, packing, and shopping for their next trip. He couldn't wait.

16

❦

June 6 - Duluth - around 3:45 a.m.

Jim spent most of the time from 3:45 until it was light outside pacing around the kitchen, dining room, and living room, waiting for daylight. He paced to keep himself awake and alert. He also drank a bottle of Mountain Dew and wished they had some coffee in the house.

Around 5:00, he grabbed a flashlight from the kitchen drawer and went back down to the basement to find the solar power station they had been using in the RV the last few years. The power station was essentially an 800-watt battery that could be recharged with a solar panel, car outlet, or by plugging it into the wall. Once charged, it could provide power through four 110V outlets, and three USB ports. The unit had been worth the money. They could use it to recharge the cochlear implant batteries, phones, devices, and, with extension cords running all over the camper, they could run fans in the bedroom and in Kelly's sleeping area at night. It wasn't the optimal situation since a nighttime trip to the bathroom could have resulted in a trip over a cord and a whole lot of mayhem on any of those nights, so Jim always warned everyone at bedtime to be very careful moving around in the night.

Jim had planned to retire the unit this year now that the RV had solar panels on the roof - making their camper's outlets operational even when they were off the grid - but if the power station was charged, he could use it now. He turned it on and saw that it was at eighty percent capacity. That was plenty for his purposes. He started to walk back towards the stairs carrying the unit by the handle, then turned back and grabbed the solar panel and the bag of charging cables. He stuck the flashlight in his pocket so he could carry everything else, so the walk up the stairs was slow and clumsy. By the time he got to the top of the stairs, he decided the power station wasn't quite ready for retirement just yet.

He set the solar panel and bag of cables down in the living room next to the coffee table and realized that he left his gun and ammunition sitting untended on the coffee table while he went downstairs. That was the first major breach of gun safety in his life and he intended it to be the last. He set the power station down, put the clips of ammunition in his pants pocket, stuffed the gun in his belt, picked up the power station, and headed upstairs.

The second floor of their house was smaller than the first floor and consisted of a family room, a bathroom, and two bedrooms. Their plan was for the girls to someday move into the bedrooms up there and have their own dorm-like space. Neither girl was interested in leaving their current bedroom yet, so Jim used one of the upstairs bedrooms as a home office. The closet in his office was used to store a lot of extra clothes and other items that Jim didn't need regularly, but didn't want to get rid of or tuck away in the basement. In the top drawer of the old dresser in the walk-in closet, he found the first item he needed – his shoulder holster for the 9mm. He slipped the shoulder holster on and secured the gun. He grabbed an old flannel shirt to throw on over the top for good measure.

There was a little bit of light coming through the window now, but the window in this room faced west, so Jim still needed the flashlight to perform his next task. He found the outlet where the TV was plugged in and pulled the plug out of the wall. He then plugged it into the power station. It took him a minute to find the remote for the TV, but he got it turned on and switched the input to the antenna. He was hoping to get some early morning news reports, preferably local, but he was out of luck. Not one station was broadcasting anything, not even PBS. The TV had nothing but static.

"What in the hell is going on out there." He said to the empty room.

It was about 5:30 a.m.

17

∾

July 1 - Outside Calgary - after lunch

After their family lunch, Joy and the girls decided to hang out in the camper and do some reading and writing. Kelly was a prolific writer of fan fiction using characters from her favorite movies and books. The only person she ever showed her writing to was Alex. Kelly had also started creating comic books on an app on her iPad. Jim hadn't seen her work, but from what he overheard, the comics involved unicorns and fairies. Alex also did some writing – not as much as Kelly – and she didn't show what she wrote to anyone.

A couple of years back, Joy suggested the girls start keeping journals, but as far as Joy and Jim knew, neither girl had taken that suggestion to heart.

Joy had already downloaded a number of books to be ready for their expected late June vacation to Newfoundland, and she was still able to read those books. Since June 7th she had been unable to download any more material from the app that provided audio books for the blind. That was a First-World problem, not life or death, but it was another annoyance she was going to have to deal with sooner or later. She usually read three to five books a week and it was going to be a big change not having anything available to read once she got through her current downloads.

While his family settled into their favorite reading and writing spots, Jim grabbed a couple bottles of water from the fridge and walked across the road to resume his conversation with Chad.

As he turned the corner and looked up the driveway into Chad's campsite, Jim could see that Chad was standing next to the picnic table manning a tabletop grill with vegetables and some sort of meat on it. "Hey Chad, you available to hang out and talk?"

Chad turned slightly to look his way and gave a little nod. "Like I said this morning, you can stop by anytime. I'm making tofu kabobs. Should be done in a couple minutes. You interested?"

"No thanks, I just had lunch with my family. If you don't mind eating in front of me, I'll stick around for a while though. I brought the waters this time. Sorry, but I don't travel with anything stronger."

"Water's fine. I've been reading my Bible all morning and it would feel weird doing that while drinking beer. Wine might be okay, but I don't have any of that."

Chad shut off his grill and put his kabobs on a plate. Jim wasn't sure if they looked good or not.

"So how far have you gotten into the Bible? My daughter, who you saw with me last night, she can get fixated on things. She once went almost a year where she read the chapter about the ten plagues in her Children's Bible every night at bedtime. I think it comforted her that God punished the bad people and saved the good people. I never tried to explain to her how killing the first-born son of every household might have taken out some good people along with the bad. I'm a Lutheran, and a believer, but the law books of the Old Testament have more holes than Swiss cheese, so I usually stick to the Gospels and the Epistles. And don't get me started on Revelation. They spend the whole New Testament telling us how much God loves us then in the end he throws just about everyone into the flaming pit. Those guys in the fourth century should have left that book on the cutting room floor."

Chad frowned. "I guess I wasn't looking for anything deeper than to finally read it from start to finish. What kind of holes are you talking about?"

They sat down while Jim thought for a few seconds. "God creates Adam and Eve. They have two sons, Cain and Abel. Cain murders Abel. God banishes him, but Cain is afraid the other people will do him harm, so God gives him a mark for protection. Where did the other people come from? If they also came from Adam and Eve wouldn't the writer mention that? Then Cain goes out and gets married. Did he marry one of his sisters? Same thing after the great flood and the only people left are Noah, his wife, their three sons, and their wives. Isn't every one of their offspring forced into a forbidden relationship with a first cousin or sibling to repopulate the land? Later Abram and Sarai are told that they will be the start of a great nation with their offspring, Isaac, but they're half-siblings, which in Leviticus, God tells Moses is a banned relationship. Lot has kids with his own daughters. Lots of incest in Genesis in my opinion. My take on the book of Genesis is that it should be taken figuratively, but not literally. That doesn't stop me from being a believer, I just think the historians and translators who put it to paper weren't very reliable. And don't get me started on the rules in Exodus 21 and 22. Most of humanity should have been executed or enslaved by now according to those rules." He paused and looked up to the sky. "Forgive me Father if those are your divine words and rules. If that's the case, I blame the translators who converted your message to English."

Chad didn't crack a smile. "Like I said, I'm just going to read it from start to finish so I can say I did it. Seemed like a good time to finally get that accomplished. I'm not looking for answers about the universe, or to find some revelation that will save America."

Jim nodded. "Sorry, I'm a bit of a talker and some subjects just get me going. Bible talk wasn't the reason I came over. You asked me this morning how we managed to get out of Duluth and across the border on the 6th and I kind of blew you off."

Chad shook his head. "I wouldn't say you blew off my question. From your reaction this morning, I can guess it might be traumatic reliving what you went through that day, and I understand if you're not ready to just spill it to some guy you met at a campground. No hard feelings on my part."

Jim nodded. "I appreciate that. But from your reaction I think you already somewhat understand what it took for us to get out. I've talked to a bunch of Canadians since we've been up here and most of them just complain about how worried they are that they won't be able to go to Florida this winter. The Walmart parking lots and campgrounds up here seem to be full of snowbirds who pass their summers up here and spend their winters in the Southern U.S. Hell, I even showed one couple some of the bullet holes in my rig, and explained how close my kids came to being killed, all that did was scare them away. The next morning, when I was taking the cover off my windshield, I found an envelope with $200 Canadian in it and a note that said *Sorry* tucked under the windshield wiper. I suspect the wife put it there during the night. I appreciated the cash, but I haven't talked to anyone up here who really understands how bad things got that day for my family. Don't get me wrong, I love the Canadian people. We've spent weeks traveling up here in years past and have always had great interactions with everyone we've met. It's just the situation right now. We've come from a war zone that shouldn't be a war zone and the people here don't know how to treat us in relation to that."

Chad set his kabob down. "Yeah. Most people when they find out I'm an American, first they say they're sorry, then they ask if I know anything about what's going on right now."

"Do you know anything about what's going on right now?" Jim was hoping for something, but not expecting anything. "I haven't found a source of information coming out of the U.S. since the 8th. After that the information flow online just dried up, at least on the sources I used to use to get news. My wife used to get news on Facebook and Twitter, but now everything out of the U.S. is blocked on those sites. I wouldn't have thought that was possible, but apparently it is. I've thought about trying to get an account on one of the fringier social media apps, but even if they have information, it probably couldn't be trusted. No point in intentionally gathering misinformation."

Chad shook his head. "I don't know anything. But I haven't really tried to find anything out either. The last few weeks I've been trying to keep my mind off of the situation as much as possible by keeping to myself and thinking about other things. I'm reading the Bible from start to finish and that's the most reading I've done since college. Haven't found any answers in there yet. Eventually I'm going to head back to the West Coast and closer to the border. There will be people there that know how to get across the border between Washington State and British Columbia. Depending on the situation, maybe I'll try to go back. I don't want to spend the winter in my camper."

"I'm with you there. That's a concern for us too." Jim paused and took a deep breath. "Look, where I come from, we keep our noses out of other people's business, but I'm trying to figure out what to do here and don't want to re-invent the wheel if you've already dealt with some of the issues that are at the top of my list. Would you mind if I pry a little bit? I won't be offended if you tell me a question is off limits. We've only known each other for a few hours."

Chad shrugged. "I haven't done much of anything but read, think, and meditate in the mountains since I got here, but go ahead and ask."

"Okay. Have you applied for asylum or refugee status or a work permit? If we're going to be here all winter, I want to be able to work and do it legally."

"Nope. I've done a few odd jobs for cash along the way. Doesn't add up to much, but I don't need much. Can't help you there."

"Got it. Have you used the health care system up here at all yet? We're going to need to get some prescriptions filled soon and I don't have a clue how anything works up here."

"Nope again. Haven't even thought about it until you mentioned it. For me, I would probably just show up at the ER and see if they treat me."

"Well, it was worth a try. I told my wife I would do some research on these issues later today. A person with first-hand experience working through an issue beats a web search as an information source ninety-nine percent of the time."

"Sorry I'm not more help. It can't be easy when you have to take care of a family in this situation."

"It's not. And it's my own fault that I've let things go this long without finding answers to my questions. I've been trying to pretend we're on vacation for the last few weeks. Fiddling while Rome burns. We're not broke or anything, and I'd like to think the authorities aren't going to deport us back to the U.S., but for my family's sake, I need to get us into the system up here so my kids can get an education and medical care."

"Sounds like you're thinking about settling down somewhere up here. Any idea where?"

Jim sighed. "That's the million-dollar question. Look, my kids are dealing with some shit. I would call it PTSD, don't know if that's what a professional would diagnose it as. Getting them some help has become our number one priority and finding a place that can help them is on my research project list. Wherever we can find help for them is where we're going to settle in. If I had to guess, that place is probably going to be a bigger city like Toronto, Montreal, Ottawa, or Vancouver. Maybe Calgary, Edmonton, or Winnipeg, but I won't know until I dig further. I've heard it's not easy for an American to move up here and work. Probably used to have lots of Americans trying to come up here and get free health care. But that was before this summer. Hopefully it will be easier now – although easy is a relative term."

It hadn't occurred to Chad to try to apply for asylum or refugee status in Canada. He was doing his best to stay off the radar of everyone, paying cash for everything and minding his own business. "You said you're not broke. I brought all the cash I had in my house and have made a little more along the way. But I don't need much and can live cheap. How long do you think you can hold out?"

"So that's a tough question. We crossed the border on the evening of the 6th. On the morning of the 7th, I showed up at a Canadian bank and opened an account, transferred as much as I could from my checking and savings accounts in the U.S., and got a debit card. Thankfully, the banking systems were still talking to each other, and I was able to transfer enough money to keep us going for quite a while. I wasn't sure if they would let me open an account up here, but apparently my money is as good as anyone's. I wanted to get a credit card, but the bank wouldn't issue one due to the uncertain situation at my permanent address. I have some CDs in the bank in the U.S. that I wanted to cash in to get that money as well, but those sales and transfers didn't go through on the 7th, and I haven't been able to access my U.S. accounts through my online banking app since then. With what we have, we could go on the way we've been going for the rest of the year, but I don't intend to spend the winter touring Canada in a camper that has duct tape covering bullet holes."

Chad had a look of awe on his face. "Wow, so you drove out of a war zone where your RV got shot up, crossed the border late in the evening, and the first thing you thought to do the next morning was to go do some banking? Your mind works different from mine, man."

Jim chuckled. "Yeah, I'm a business consultant, or at least I was. Some of my clients may have considered me a bit of a Negative Nelly, for lack of a better term. When clients would come to me with a great plan, it was my job to help them realize that vision, but also to help them see where the landmines were along the path to their destination. My first instinct in most situations is to try to find the potholes in the road and patch them up. As soon as we were safely across the border, I knew we were going to be here a while and I feared our U.S. credit card wasn't going to be useful for long. We needed to be able to buy food and gas, so securing a source of cash was the first obstacle. Immediately after we left the bank, I bought a new cell phone on a Canadian service plan. Again, insurance in case our U.S. plan went belly up with no warning. Charged the phone on my U.S. credit card, which stopped working sometime on the 9th, but the card worked long enough for me to charge like $300 of groceries and over $4,000 of RV repairs that morning. When I realized it wasn't working any more, I tried the 800 number on the card, but could not reach a human to try to keep it activated. Their loss, I would have kept paying it if I could have kept using it. Since they won't let me charge any more, they don't get paid for the outstanding balance. Pretty sure maintaining my outstanding credit rating isn't worth a damn for anything right now."

Chad laughed, "When I got up this morning, talking about credit ratings didn't cross my mind. Mine isn't bad either, by the way."

Jim laughed along, "Yeah, I didn't have credit rating on my Canada Day Bingo card either, but what are you going to do."

Jim stopped laughing. "I hate to get serious again, but this morning you said some things that touched on the political situation in the U.S. before the 6th. You said that what happened might be a conspiracy all the way up to the White House. I get that what you said was speculation. Neither of us knows who was involved in planning what happened. But just for the sake of this discussion, let's say this was coordinated all the way to the top. I follow politics enough to know that the guy in the White House, he lost the popular vote, but nobody had enough Electoral College votes, so the House of Representatives made him President. His party also controls the Senate and the House of Representatives. He used the military to quell all those protests after the House handed him the Presidency. He pardoned all those people who beat up on the Capitol Police in 2021. They won. They control everything - all three branches of the government. The economy was already tanking from cutting off trade with Mexico while they were fighting the cartels, but this has to have shut just about everything down. Why weaken the country when there are external threats to national security? It doesn't make sense to me. We're lucky the Russians have been so chewed up in Ukraine, or this would be a great opportunity for them to annex Alaska."

Chad thought for a while. "I don't know, man. Pre-emptive strike to make sure they keep control? Manufacture another crisis that needs a strong-man in power? Just plain hatred of people who live in cities? Urban areas haven't supported the guy. Maybe he just decided to let his supporters work out their anger and get a little payback for him. He's made it clear that anyone who does his bidding, no matter how many laws they break, will be pardoned for their crimes. At this point it isn't like fear of a long prison term is a deterrent for his supporters."

Jim looked down at the table and spoke slowly. "My dad was a Marine and was proud to have served. I was raised to love our country - warts and all. Growing up it felt like we were all on the same team as Americans even if we didn't agree on some of the divisive issues. It doesn't feel that way to me anymore. Powerful people who should be inspiring us to work together are intentionally dividing us. Now, you can pretty regularly know how a judge is going to rule based on who appointed them before the case is even argued. When is the last time you were surprised by a ruling out of one of the Southern circuits or by the Supreme Court? Hell, the Supreme Court now makes up fact patterns that don't exist just so they can change the laws faster. Our congressional districts are so gerrymandered that you know which party is going to win the election before any votes are cast. And no politician can admit to compromising with the other side or they'll lose a primary. While I didn't see June 6th coming, I felt like close to half of our country was no longer on the same team. But I thought that still left a lot of good people who saw other Americans as friends and teammates, not enemies. Even someone as prone to look for the warning signs as I am, I didn't think something like this could happen. Once they called off the Insurrection Act and sent all the troops to the Southern border, life had started to get back towards a semblance of normal. I still expected isolated pockets of political violence, sure, but a potentially nationwide coordinated attack, no way. I thought the loony politicians calling for all out civil war or national divorce were crazy. Was one team going to wear red hats and the other team blue hats and just walk the streets hunting each other? Turns out they weren't that loony; I just had rose-colored glasses on."

Chad looked at Jim for a couple seconds. "Sounds like you pay a bit more attention to politics than you said a minute ago." Jim shrugged and Chad continued. "I think most people don't pay attention to all the hate and nastiness, either because they don't want to believe it exists or because they have other problems to deal with in their daily lives. Now it's front and center in every American's life. We've got to hope the good guys hold out and the bad guys learn their lesson when this is all done."

"You're right that I have been paying attention, but paying attention without taking any action. I don't remember exactly how the saying goes, something like – all it takes for evil to flourish is for good people to do nothing – and too many people like me just watched all the nastiness without speaking out against it. Hate in America has become a spectator sport. Hell, I even did business with one of the biggest pushers of hate, just to get the convenience of satellite internet on my RV. You got involved and helped to stand up to the evil, but I just watched and kept my head down. I can tell myself I didn't want to put my family at risk of some random crazy person, of which there are way too many out there, but look where we are now. Maybe if a couple million other Americans like me had stood up and said no more to what was happening, this could have been stopped before it came to civil war."

Chad stood up and started to clean up his lunch remains. "You were ready when the shit hit the fan because you were paying attention. You got your family out. You said that was blessing enough, and it's going to have to be." He yawned. "I didn't get much sleep last night and could use a nap. I still want to hear about what you saw on the 6th if you feel up to talking about it. My last intel from the U.S. was when I was around Vancouver, and I left there on June 10th. And even that was second and third hand stories from people who told me what they heard from other people. What I heard then was pretty dark, semi-trucks flipped on their sides to block the roads and shooting anyone who tried to get around them. Flying drones with explosives into populated areas. That kind of stuff. But I don't know if anything I heard was real. I understand if you don't want to relive all the gory details, but if you do feel up to sharing, I'm really interested, and it might help me in figuring out what I'm going to do next."

Jim got up to leave. "Tell you what. Block out a chunk of time this evening and I'll tell you what happened that day – or at least as much as I can. Start to finish. It's going to take a while."

Jim picked up his water bottle and headed back to his camper.

18

June 6 - Duluth - around 5:30 a.m.

Jim unplugged the TV and carried the power station down to the living room. He peeked out the curtain to the street out front. Everything looked like a normal morning, other than the streetlight being out – and there was enough daylight now that the streetlight might have turned off by itself even if the power was working.

He wasn't sure just what was going on – maybe there was an innocent explanation for the power outage, cell service outage, and TV stations being out – but the combination of those things with the sirens, gunfire, and explosions during the night, led Jim to think he might want to hope for the best, but plan for the worst. With that in mind, he went back downstairs and started hauling up all of the family's empty suitcases.

Jim carried his suitcase up to his office. As quickly and efficiently as he could without forgetting something important, he tried to pack enough of his clothes to get him through a couple weeks on the road. He also packed toiletries, charging cords, and electronics. He filled a large suitcase and a backpack with clothing. A second backpack held his iPad, chargers, earbuds, toothbrush, toothpaste, electric razor, notepads and pens, some washcloths, and a towel from the upstairs bathroom. He tried to remember what items he had on his packing list the previous year for their annual RV trip and thought he had everything covered.

After packing the bags, he strapped his watch around his left wrist. It was now almost 6:30.

As he was walking out of his office, he stopped one more time. He didn't know where they might be going or for how long, so he pulled out his work bag and shoved his laptop, mouse, power cable, and portable extra monitors into the bag. Maybe he was going to need to use the satellite internet in the RV for work. Heck, he might just get to write it off on his taxes this year.

Jim set down all the packed bags near the back door, opened the garage door, pointed the flashlight in, and took a peek. The car was sitting right where he parked it and nothing in the garage looked out of place. He turned off the flashlight and looked at the big garage door – no bullet holes in it, no light showing through where it shouldn't.

He pulled the bags from inside the house into the garage and set them down near the man-door next to the big door. He went back to the house door and made sure it was locked behind him and he had his keys in his pocket. Damn – forgot the keys to the RV. He went back into the house and got the RV keys off the hook by the door. Checking again to make sure the door was locked behind him before making his way to the door to the outside.

Before opening the door, he unclipped the strap that secured the gun in his shoulder holster, pulled out the gun and loaded it. He made sure the safety was on and slid it back into the holster. Then he listened for a few seconds, opened the door, and eased his way out, trying to look everywhere at the same time. The morning was quiet, some birds singing in the distance, but no sounds of human activity at all. Jim walked the fifty feet down the driveway and looked up the street – nothing happening there. He came back into the driveway and stepped off onto the gravel area next to the driveway where he parked his RV. He did a slow walk all the way around the RV looking for any sign that the vehicle was hit by stray gunfire during the night. All six tires looked good, no broken windows or lights, everything looked to be in good shape.

Jim looked around his front yard, scanning for any movement. Seeing nothing out of the ordinary, he opened the RV door and stepped inside. He opened the curtains on the big windows over the table and the couch so he could see up the street through the window over the dinette area on the driver's side and he had a great view of his front yard and house through the big window over the couch on the passenger side. His neighbors had installed a solid wood privacy fence a few years back so they wouldn't have to stare at the RV from their dining room table, but he had pulled the RV forward from its winter resting spot so the dining area window was now just beyond the end of the fence. As long as he checked out the windows on both sides frequently, nobody should be able to sneak up on him. He was starting to feel like his paranoia was overkill, but reminded himself that there was what sounded like a war not that far away only a few hours ago. Better safe, than dead.

Now that he was in the RV, he had access to the satellite internet. He flipped the system on and pulled his phone out of his pocket. His phone automatically joined the network and he punched the Apple News app. Local news would be better, but it was unlikely the Duluth News Tribune would have much of anything posted this early. The top headline on Apple News was from the Washington Post – "Power Outages Nationwide, Foul Play Suspected" – there was a sub-headline that said breaking in red letters. He scanned the story. Power outages were reported in a number of different states during the night, it was suspected that power infrastructure had been attacked – possibly revenge attacks by the cartels in response to U.S. military incursions into Mexico, possibly by white nationalists - there were reports of explosions and shootings in some of the locations, police may have come under attack in parts of the country. The facts were still unclear. The story made it sound like orchestrated chaos all over the country.

"Holy shit," Jim muttered as he tried the app for the local newspaper.

As expected, there was nothing posted more recently than the previous evening on the local newspaper app – a story about a school district referendum that would be on the ballot in November. Jim closed that app and sat back to think. It seemed like the events in Duluth that he observed during the night matched up pretty closely with the story from the Washington Post. He didn't want to jump to conclusions, but it probably wasn't just a coincidence. But why Duluth? It wasn't exactly a metropolis. It was highly unlikely the Mexican drug cartels were attacking the infrastructure and shooting it out with the police in Duluth, Minnesota. Even in his current paranoid state of mind, that was a bridge too far for Jim. He thought about recent days. *Had he seen anything suspicious or unusual? Nothing came to mind. Wait, there was that really odd letter to the editor in last Sunday's newspaper.* At the time he thought the person who wrote it was a little too deep down the Q/white Christian nationalist rabbit hole. He had read the letter three times without being able to discern what the writer was trying to advocate for, but now he wondered if it was simply a signal mixed in with triggering words and gibberish; the letter had mentioned D-Day.

He looked at his watch again - almost 7:00; Time to get Joy moving and make a plan. She can go on Facebook and find out more of what's going on locally - if anyone else has been posting anything.

19

July 1 - Outside Calgary - early afternoon

Jim slipped into the RV and looked to his right. The girls were in their favorite reading spots – Alex on the couch, Kelly up in her sleeping area – completely focused on whatever books they were reading. He was proud to have raised a couple of kids who loved to read every day. He hoped they were lost in the worlds of their stories so they could spend some time not thinking about the here and now. He quietly slipped back to the bedroom without disturbing them. Joy was sitting on the bed, headphones in her ears, with a notebook in her lap. She paused her book when he came in.

Speaking quietly so the girls couldn't hear, she said, "I'm making notes about the girls for when we can meet with a psychologist. I don't want to forget to mention anything important. What are you up to?"

He was grabbing his iPad off the counter by the bed. "I'm going to take my iPad over near the office and do that research. Fingers crossed the Wi-Fi works over there. Don't know if the office will be open, but do you need anything if they are?"

She shook her head, "No. Just remember you're there to do research, not to make friends. Stay focused." She had a very serious look on her face as she said this.

Jim saluted. "Yes, ma'am. I will return by dinner time with my assignment completed or I will walk the plank." He turned and started to walk out, then stopped and turned back. "What time is dinner tonight?"

Now she smiled, "Be back by 5:00, smartass."

Jim quickly slipped back past the girls and out the door, heading for the campground office.

20

June 6 - Duluth - around 7 a.m.

Jim locked up the RV and made his way through the garage and into the house, leaving his packed bags in the garage and locking all the doors behind him. At the bedroom door he listened for a couple seconds, but didn't hear any noise coming from the room. He opened the door and peeked in, expecting to see Joy sitting up reading an audiobook on her phone, but she was fast asleep between the girls on the bed. He hoped she had fallen asleep quickly after their last conversation, because she was going to need to be fully functioning for at least the next couple of hours.

Jim leaned over Kelly and gently shook Joy by the shoulder. She jumped and woke up both girls with her startled reaction. They both then were similarly startled. This was not how Jim was planning for their day to start, but at least everybody was now awake.

Once she got her bearings, Kelly asked if she could go back to her own room. She was still sleepy and wanted to be in her own bed. Jim said she could, and, cuddling her Pinkie Bear, she went across the hall and shut her door.

Alex was still too tired to move, so she just rolled over and went back to sleep right there. Since there was no fear of having her overhear the conversation, Jim started talking.

"Sorry to hit you with this before you've had a chance to wake up, but the situation may be even more serious than we thought last night. Not only is the power out, but we have no cell service here and none of the local TV networks are broadcasting anything. I read a news story that said there were organized attacks on infrastructure all over the country during the night last night. Power stations were hit, shootouts with police. I'm thinking they may have also taken out the cell towers and the antenna farm here in town. Don't know how else we wouldn't have any antenna TV or cell service. So, I was thinking maybe we start our vacation a little early and head north today. With the satellite internet on the RV, we can work on the road from anywhere and we can take our time getting to the ferry dock in Nova Scotia. Maybe even find an RV park with a pool and a nice playground and stay there for a while. The girls would love having a pool for days."

Joy was getting out of bed while he talked. As she got dressed, she wasn't sold on leaving town right away. "With the solar power and the satellite internet, can't we just stay in the RV here in our driveway for a few days until we see if the power is going to come back on? Why do we need to hurry up and leave town?"

"I don't know that we do need to leave town, but the news said the attacks were all over the country and I don't really want to spend the next few nights cowering here hiding out from stray bullets and explosions like last night. I'd like to be somewhere that I can go to sleep without a gun under my pillow."

"Do you have a loaded gun on you right now?" Her tone was accusatory. "We agreed you would never have either of your guns loaded around the girls."

Jim pulled open his flannel shirt. "It is loaded and the safety is on. I'm planning to do a little recon once you're up and we have a plan. And I'm not going out there without being ready for anything after what we heard last night."

"Please unload it now. Give me a few minutes to get dressed."

He nodded. "You should probably wear jeans and something with sleeves. You may have to be outside some today."

Jim went into the kitchen and grabbed a granola bar out of the cupboard. Just a little something to keep him going for a little while. He wasn't feeling tired now, but was concerned that a long day of driving in the RV might be a problem. He dug around in the cupboard and found a couple of bottles of 5-hour Energy that had probably been there for at least three years, decided beggars can't be choosers, and put them on the counter to hopefully remember them later.

Joy came into the kitchen and grabbed a cold coffee out of the drawer in the refrigerator. Jim had forgotten about them during the night when he had needed a pick-me-up, but now didn't want the caffeine rush that would inevitably be followed by a crash. "Did you unload your gun?"

"As far as you know." This was Jim's way of saying "I'm not going to do what you asked because I think you're wrong, but I'm not going to tell you you're wrong." Joy understood the meaning of the phrase.

Joy sighed, "Just don't shoot either of us and please unload it when you're around the girls."

"I will if I can. Now can you join me in the RV? Bring your iPad. I want you to check your Facebook account to see if you can find out anything about what's going on around here."

Joy went to the living room and grabbed her iPad. "If we don't have power, internet, or cell service, what makes you think anyone else will be able to post stuff?"

"I've been up all night thinking. It's unlikely the entire area is without power and cell service. Nobody could possibly attack every significant part of the infrastructure around here in one night without a force of hundreds and some damn good intelligence. Somebody still has to be able to post stuff. You have Facebook friends all over town, maybe some areas didn't get hit or maybe someone went out and checked around and saw something last night then found a place where they could get on-line to post about it. It's worth a try."

As they headed to the door, Jim turned back and looked at Joy, "Okay, just stay behind me and lock the doors behind us."

"You're not going to whip your gun out and cover me while I sprint to the camper, are you? You might be taking things a bit too seriously."

"Better safe than dead." Jim went out the door and Joy followed.

Once in the RV, Joy sat down at the table and started looking at her iPad. Jim was scanning out the two big windows. "I'm going out to take the privacy cover off the windshield. Do you want me to put up the curtain, so the sun doesn't get you?" The RV was facing east, and the rising sun would be coming through the windshield directly into the living/dining area, but Jim wanted the cover off so he could see directly in front of them. It was a blind spot in his security right now.

"If you want me to be able to see anything, yes."

Jim hung up the curtain that they sometimes used to divide the driver's cab from the living area. Then he went out and pulled off the vinyl windshield cover. With that out of the way, they could move out pretty quickly if the time came to leave. He stuffed the cover into the rear storage compartment and came back into the camper.

Joy was waiting for him impatiently. "You have to see this." She was holding out her iPad.

"What am I looking at?" He didn't use social media and wanted to make sure he understood what she was showing him. He took the iPad from her and looked at the screen.

"One of the people I'm friends with (she made air quotes as she said friends) is extremely political and was way into the stop the steal stuff. I think he went to D.C. for January 6th. He's blocked just about all of our other high school classmates, but for some reason hasn't blocked me. I usually find the stuff he posts entertaining in a scary way, but look what he posted a couple hours ago."

"I know who you're talking about. You've read his posts to me many times." Jim looked closer. The post, which was excessively capitalized and oddly punctuated, said:

"HAPPY D-DAY LIBS! GET READY TO HAVE YOUR CITIES STORMED LIKE NORMANDY BEACHES!! THERES NO PLACE TO HIDE. RETRIBUTION IS COMING!!!"

Jim was used to the guy's posts being a source of humor, so he wasn't sure how to take what he just read. "Well, he's always been a little loony. Maybe it's a scare tactic and all bluster. But if he knows something and he's telegraphing it out, then we need to consider getting out of town fast." He pulled out his phone and took a photo of the post.

Out of the corner of his eye, Jim saw movement in the neighbor's driveway to the north. He looked out the window over the dinette and saw that the widow who lived next door had just wandered down her driveway beyond the end of her privacy fence. She was just looking around and hadn't seemed to have noticed that Jim and Joy were in the camper. "I'm going to go talk to Nancy next door. See if you can find anything from a more reliable news source."

"Okay. But Jim, don't get chatty out there. If we need to leave, we still have a lot to do to get ready."

He leaned down and gave her a kiss on the head. "10-4 babe. I will keep it short and sweet."

Jim went out around the front of the camper making sure to yell "Hello Nancy," from a good distance before he started walking across the grass between the two driveways. He didn't want to surprise or scare his neighbor. She might also be armed and jumpy this morning.

Nancy was in her late 70's and had been widowed for a while. Jim didn't know her well, just occasional chats in the yard when they were both outside – mostly about the weather, kids and grandkids, and random neighborhood gossip. She seemed a little out of sorts this morning.

"My power is out and my phone doesn't work. I was going to drive to my son's house, but my garage door won't open."

Jim nodded. "I can help you get your garage door open. Did you try calling on a landline or just on your cell phone?"

She looked like she was trying to remember. "My son had me cancel my landline right after my husband passed. Said it was a waste of money. Can you help me right now? I want to get going."

Jim heard some voices behind him in the distance and snapped his head around quickly, his right hand starting toward the gun hanging below his left shoulder. He relaxed when he saw it was another couple from the neighborhood who looked to be loading up the back of their SUV.

Jim turned back to Nancy and said, "Give me one minute to talk to Carl and Julie and I'll be right back to get you out of your garage." He turned and trotted across the cul-de-sac hoping the gun wasn't swinging out from under his open flannel shirt.

Carl and Julie were in their early 60's and seemed to be pretty physically active. Jim and Carl had spoken at length maybe a dozen times over the years, but Jim didn't know Carl's politics or much other than he was a good neighbor, had an expensive snow blower, and they could always make small talk without any problem.

Carl saw him coming and said, "Good morning."

"Hey Carl. Looks like you're packing up to head out. This might sound a little crazy to you, but Joy and I are thinking about heading for the Canadian border this morning and I think it might be safer to travel in a group. Wondering if you might be interested."

Carl looked at Jim with a curious expression. "Do you know something I don't?"

"I don't know what you know, but I assume you heard the sirens, gunfire and explosions last night after the power went out." Carl nodded and Jim continued. "I saw a Washington Post story this morning that said power infrastructure was attacked all over the country and police were under attack." He pulled out his phone and showed it to Carl. "Joy saw this on Facebook this morning."

Carl read the D-Day post and ran his free hand through his hair. "Holy shit. Do you know the person who posted this?"

Jim nodded. "Unfortunately, yes, I've met him. I don't know if it's real or just a scare tactic. He was there on January 6th and is a true believer. I wouldn't be surprised if he knows people in militias or is a militia member himself."

Carl handed back the phone shaking his head. "Julie and I are going to finish packing up and head to our cabin in Wisconsin. It has electricity and internet access, but no cell service. If the power is out there, it has a generator we can use. If what you say is true, our kids will know to go to the cabin and meet up with us there. That's what we have to do. I really hope you make it to Canada."

Jim was disappointed but wasn't expecting Carl to just go along with him. "Can you do me a favor? Can I enter my contact info into your phone so you can send me an e-mail and let me know when you get to your cabin? And maybe let me know what things looked like on the way there too. I have the satellite dish on my RV, so I can get e-mails even without cell service."

Carl nodded. "Sure, and give me your phone so I can give you my info too."

They traded phones and entered their contact information.

Jim stuck out his hand to shake Carl's. "Good luck to you and Julie. Stay safe out there." Then he pulled open his flannel shirt to reveal his gun. "And if you have weapons you can carry with you, now would be a good time to pack them in the car."

"That was the first thing I packed. Now we've got to go. Good luck to you, Joy, and your kids."

Jim turned and trotted back to Nancy's driveway.

"Okay, let's get that garage door opened."

They went into the garage through the side door and Jim looked over at the main door where he could see light coming through two small holes about six inches apart on the right side of the door as he was facing it from inside the garage.

"Nancy, could you come over here for a second?" He crouched down and pointed at the holes. "Have you noticed those before?"

She looked at where he was pointing and said, "No, the door didn't have any holes in it before."

Jim turned on the flashlight on his phone. "I promise, this won't take more than a couple minutes." He put his back to the garage door and walked straight through to the back of the garage along the path the bullets would have traveled if they had gone straight in. He flashed the light along the back wall, and it didn't take long to see where they were embedded in the back wall of the garage. Fortunately, Nancy's car was not in the path they took. He called Nancy over and pointed to the bullets in the wall.

"If you didn't hear it, there was some shooting off to the East last night after the power went out. Looks like a couple of stray bullets came through your garage and ended up here."

She looked horrified. "I should call the police. And my insurance company. I need to talk to my son."

Jim nodded. "I'll show you how to unhook your garage door from the electric opener. Your son lives close by, right?"

She nodded as Jim pulled the handle that freed the door from the mechanism. Jim then lifted the door open, and the light poured in. "Okay Nancy, please just drive straight to your son's house and don't stop for anybody. I'll close the door after you pull out, but anyone can open it now. If you need to lock the door that leads into your house, you should do that before you go."

Nancy got in her car and backed out of her driveway. Jim shut the garage door. He wondered if he would ever see her again.

Jim hurried back to the RV to see if Joy had learned anything more. As he walked between the driveways, Carl and Julie drove by and he waved to them.

21

July 1 - Outside Calgary - mid afternoon

Jim arrived at the campground office and saw that it was still open. He hoped there wouldn't be too much traffic today since it was a holiday, and sat down on a bench on the porch. He turned on his iPad and got connected to the campground Wi-Fi. The signal seemed to be strong, but the only way to find out was to try to open up a web page. After typing "asylum Canada" into the browser, he started working his way through the maze of information on the Government of Canada's website. Within minutes he was lost and confused trying to follow the information while wishing he had brought paper and a pen to write notes. He decided to see if the campground office had some scrap paper and a pen they would let him use.

Upon entering the office, he was greeted by the same woman who had been working the previous evening. She wished him a Happy Canada Day and he returned the greeting. Before he could ask for some paper, she started talking.

"So, I noticed when you checked in last night that you're from Minnesota. Didn't say anything last night 'cause you looked pretty tired, but are you doing okay?"

This wasn't the question Jim was expecting, and he appreciated it. "We have good days and bad days. It looks like we're probably going to be in Canada for a while and I need to figure out how we accomplish that. Any chance you know anything about filing for asylum? I need to be able to work to support my family and my kids need healthcare services. After what we went through to get to the border, I can't take my kids back down there until I know the U.S. is safe again."

She smiled, "Just so happens that one of our regular guests works for the government in immigration services. He comes here every year. Real nice guy, Brad something that starts with an L. Give me about ten minutes and I'll get you his contact information."

"Really?" Jim felt a wave of relief. He really needed help to get through this process and maybe he was going to be thrown a lifeline. "Take your time. I'll wait outside. I really appreciate your help."

"I'm happy to help you and your family. This country took my parents in many years ago when they needed a safe place to live. We should be able to do the same thing for your family. I'll be out when I find Brad's information."

Jim went back outside and sat down on the bench. He started up his iPad and as he went to open his browser app, he was suddenly and uncontrollably overcome with emotion. Tears began streaming down his cheeks as he tried to get control of himself. He wiped at his eyes and looked around, hoping nobody was seeing his emotional breakdown. The thought that he should be worried if some strangers he would never see again might catch him showing emotion brought a little crying chuckle out of him. He had a few minutes of self-reflection.

What the hell is wrong with you? Is it your Lutheran upbringing or your dad hammering on about not showing weakness that you can't show any emotion when other people might be around? Nobody is going to care if you sit here and cry after everything your family has gone through. Then he had the thought that broke the crying spell. *Kelly always says she's never seen you cry, maybe you should take a selfie to show her later.*

That last thought got him laughing instead of crying. He wiped his face on his shirt and went back to his research. On the search engine, he typed "psychological services kids Canada," and started sorting through the results. Not knowing where his family might end up made this search more informational than substantive, but he wanted to have an idea where they might be able to find specialized services for kids with PTSD when they met with immigration services. He had found a couple of promising leads and taken screenshots of their addresses and phone numbers when the office door opened, and the campground owner came out.

She started talking immediately, "We lucked out. Brad answered his phone, even on the holiday he answered, and we had a nice conversation about you and your family. He says the rules have been changed because of the number of desperate Americans coming across the border and you will be better served if you go to an office farther from the border." She pulled a piece of paper out of her pocket. "There's an address in Calgary on here and a phone number. You should call the number tomorrow when the office is open and ask for Sheila. Brad is going to let her know you will be calling, so maybe wait until 9 or 10 before you call. Brad said Sheila will help you with the process and help you figure out where you might want to settle down until you can go back to Minnesota. He said you will like working with her." She held out the piece of paper.

Jim stood up and took the paper. He read it over twice while gathering himself. He was working at holding back the tears and was succeeding this time, but barely. Eventually, he looked up. Now he saw her name tag.

"Angel? Wow are you ever. I can't thank you enough. Obviously, we'll be checking out tomorrow morning, but I promise my family will not forget how much you helped us. Once we get our lives figured out, we will be back."

She smiled, "You don't owe me anything. All I did was make a phone call to a friend. I'll be happy to have your business in the future, but don't feel like you need to do anything special to pay me back. You take care of your family."

Jim lurched forward and gave Angel a big hug. Now he was crying openly. "I have to go tell my wife. Thank you so much."

He turned and hurried back towards his RV.

22

June 6 - Duluth - around 7:30 a.m.

Back in the RV, Joy had a lot to tell. She had seen Facebook posts from all over the country that mentioned chaos, including a group of armed men shooting people in the streets in Madison, police cars on fire in St. Paul, buildings burning in Milwaukee, and a local post that said the mall in Duluth was on fire. After years of thinking social media was nothing but a useless time burglar, Jim finally saw some usefulness in Joy's large friend network.

"If we decide to leave, we can't go past the mall. Whoever started that fire might still be there." Her voice was a little shaky.

Jim thought for a minute. "I think you should go pack and help the girls pack as much as they can. Enough clothes to last a while and any food we can bring in the camper." He walked over and turned on the refrigerator. "It'll take a while for the fridge in here to get cold, but by the time you're all packed we should be able to load up."

She looked right at him, eyes narrowed. "And what are you going to do while we're packing?"

"I'm going to do a little recon mission. I'll take the car and drive up the highway to see if there's a clear way out of town. Maybe we'll get lucky and Highway 53 is open, but we won't know without checking. I'd rather find out in the car by myself than in the RV with you and the kids."

"No Jim. What if something happens to you? What are we supposed to do then?"

Jim took her hand, "We don't have any good options right now. Nancy just went to go stay with her son. Carl and Julie are headed to their cabin in Wisconsin. If all of our neighbors are going places, there are probably going to be lots of other people doing the same thing. I'll be armed and I'll be as careful as I can, but we need to know what's going on beyond our neighborhood to make a decision."

"I'm scared, Jim."

"I am too. I don't know if it's more dangerous to leave or to stay. I don't know how to figure out what the best way out of town is. I just keep running through the worst-case scenarios in my head and I really want don't want it to come to what my mind can think up. The thought of being trapped here with two handguns and thirty-two bullets when a horde of Vikings with AR-15's and body armor shows up to rape and pillage is my worst case. I don't want to have to use the last four bullets on us to save us from an even worse fate. After what happened to those families in Israel in 2023, we know there are worse things than a quick death. I promise I will be really careful, and I'll turn around if I run into anything that looks remotely dangerous out there."

She was visibly shaking now. "Oh God. Don't let it come to that. You need to keep our girls safe, Jim."

He hugged her tightly. "I will, honey. Every decision we make from here on is about protecting them. So let's go in the house and get started on packing. I'm going to grab my binoculars and head out. Be sure to grab all the documents in the cabinet in the bedroom. We'll need our passports and birth certificates. And if you have time, maybe grab a storage tote from the basement and fill it with their favorite books. Kelly won't make it very long without her Bible and her *Complete Idiot's Guide to the Bible.*"

They left the RV and Jim locked it behind them just to be safe. They went through the garage and into the house. The girls were still sleeping so Joy grabbed the first suitcase and went into their bedroom to start packing. Alex didn't even notice, she was still asleep on the bed.

23

July 1 - Outside Calgary - later afternoon

Jim got back to the RV and, thankfully, the girls were still engrossed in their books. He wordlessly walked back to the bedroom where Joy was ready with a stern gaze.

"You weren't gone long enough to have done all that research. Did you give up or was the Wi-Fi no good?"

He grinned, "I made a new friend and she may have been sent from heaven. She got us an appointment at an immigration office in Calgary for tomorrow."

Joy was stunned. "Really. How?"

Jim explained what had just taken place at the campground office without neglecting any details. Then he jumped onto the bed and he and Joy embraced.

"Tomorrow morning, we head to Calgary. I'll call the immigration office around 10 to see if we can get in there tomorrow. If not, we park at the nearest Walmart until we can get in. We should get all our documents together so we're ready for tomorrow."

Joy, always thinking ahead, moved on to the next important problem. "What about finding a psychologist for the girls? Did you look into that?"

Jim nodded. "I did some research and took some screenshots of some places that looked promising. But I think we need to handle the immigration part of it first in case that limits where we can go. I'm feeling hopeful because there were a lot of options and they were in all of the main cities. Think about where you might want to settle down if we have to stay in Canada for more than the school year, but they give us the choice of where to live. I would prefer to stay away from Quebec since I don't speak French. Winnipeg is closest to Minnesota, but Toronto might be okay. Vancouver could also be an option. Or maybe you would want to try Nova Scotia, maybe Halifax? This could be an opportunity to just pick a place to live and start from scratch. That might be a good list to start, a list of what you want our new hometown to offer."

Joy grabbed her notebook, turned to a blank page, and handed it to Jim. "Start writing this down." He looked around for something to write with and she handed him a pen. "A good school for the girls, PTSD counseling, medical care, safe streets, affordable rents because we are not living in this camper all winter, a place to park the RV, you can find a job, I can find a job, maybe not too close to the U.S. border just in case, near some national parks we can visit. Now you think of some."

It took Jim a minute to finish writing the list Joy had just rambled off. He was suddenly feeling drained from all the emotional ups and downs the day had thrown at him. "How about I think about it and add some later? My brain is not the sharpest right now. I could use a thirty-minute break from thinking."

She poked him in the side. "Just because you can't think of as many as me, doesn't mean you have to give up. You do plenty of other good things – thinking just isn't one of your best skills."

"You got me there. But I did make lunch, so you get to make dinner. I'm going to go back outside and sit in the shade and just decompress for a while. Let me know when it's time to eat. Can't wait to see what you make."

With that, he hopped off of the bed and slipped back outside without disturbing the girls.

24

June 6 - Duluth - around 8 a.m.

While Joy packed in the bedroom, Jim grabbed his binoculars out of the kitchen drawer. Then he went back downstairs and opened up the gun safe. He picked up the revolver and the box with twelve rounds and headed back upstairs.

Back in the bedroom, Joy was packing quickly. Jim watched for a few seconds, worried that she would forget something important in her rush, but they didn't have time to tag-team the job, so he hoped she was in a good enough frame of mind for the task at hand. He walked over close to her and showed her the revolver and the box of bullets.

"I'm going to put these in the cabinet next to the microwave. Top shelf. Do you remember how to load it and get it ready to shoot?"

She paused, looked at the gun, and shuddered a little. "Please don't let it come to that Jim. I don't want to have to shoot anyone and I'm not shooting anyone I love."

He looked around to make sure Kelly wasn't within earshot to hear what Joy had just said. "If someone tries to break in while I'm gone, get the girls and hide in our bathroom with the door locked. Put anything you can in front of the door. I won't be gone more than thirty minutes. Here, I'll put the gun in the bathroom closet on the top shelf. Don't load it unless you have to."

He went into the bathroom and put the gun in the closet. Then he came back and gave her a hug. "I'll be quick and careful. I love you."

As he was leaving, he stopped to give Alex a hug. She barely stirred in the bed. He went across the hall and opened the door to Kelly's room. She was sleeping with her Pinkie Bear held tightly. He gave her a little kiss on the head and shut her door gently on his way out.

As he headed back through the house to the garage, he offered a brief prayer, "God, please protect my family today and give us the strength to face whatever we encounter. Amen."

He grabbed the binoculars then stopped and left his wallet on the counter. No sense in letting the bad guys know where you live if they get you. Then he headed out the door, making sure it was locked behind him.

He got in the car and hit the button to open the garage door before remembering that wasn't going to do anything. He got back out of the car and pulled the cord to release the door from the chain, then carefully lifted it and looked around – still quiet out front. As he was headed back to the car, he looked around the garage to see if there was anything he might find useful on this mission. Ladder, no, chainsaw, no, crowbar, sure, tennis racquet, no, baseball bat, yes, nail gun, no, hammer, yes. He went to the tool box and grabbed his box cutter. After tossing all the items onto the passenger seat he started the car and backed out. He quickly hopped out and shut the garage door behind him before leaving. No sense in bringing attention to the fact that he wasn't home.

They lived on the end of a cul-de-sac, so Jim only had one way out of the neighborhood. He drove slowly up the street looking for any activity. There were fifteen houses between Jim's driveway and the main road. At the third house on the left, the woman who lived there stepped off the porch and waved both of her arms over her head as Jim's car approached. Jim couldn't remember her name – he cursed himself for being a crappy neighbor. Jim rolled down his window and stopped the car in front of her house.

She walked up to the edge of her yard, but didn't step into the street so there was about twenty feet between them. She spoke loudly to cover the distance and the sound of his engine.

"Carl told me you're going to drive to Canada. He said you saw some scary stuff online and think we need to get out of town. Is that right?"

"I'm not 100 percent sure we're going to drive to Canada, but it's one option right now. I'm headed up the highway to see how things look first."

"Would you take your camper if you go?"

He nodded, "Yeah that would be the plan. We were going to Canada in a couple of weeks anyway for our summer road trip."

She took a couple steps closer, "When would you be leaving if you go?"

"Hopefully this morning some time. I'd like to get across the border before dark. My wife is packing right now."

She continued moving closer to the car, "Can we follow you? I need about an hour to go to my daughter's house. I want her to come with too. We have family in Ontario we can stay with, but I would feel better travelling in a group. My husband wants to stay here, but I'll get him to change his mind."

Jim smiled, "Yes. The more of us, the better. Do you have any guns you can bring and are any of you any good with them?"

She smiled now, too. "I'll drive and Chuck can literally ride shotgun. We won't be sitting ducks out there."

"Great. I'll stop here when I get back. We definitely won't be ready to leave for at least an hour. And if you find more people who want to come along, just invite them."

Jim waved and headed up the street. He was a few houses from the main road when he noticed another one of his neighbors out in his front yard. The man was setting up a campaign sign for the President that had last been in his yard during the previous election, but Jim remembered the sign being taken down soon after the inauguration.

Jim knew that he and his neighbor did not share the same political views based on the candidates his neighbor was proud to support with lawn signs over the years, but they had never had any negative interactions – mostly just waving as Jim drove by or chatting about generalities if they ran into each other on the street. Jim wasn't sure how today's conversation was going to go, so he quickly pulled the gun out of its holster and held it across his lap below window level as he stopped the car and initiated the conversation.

"Hey Norm, you know the President is constitutionally limited to his current term. He can't run for re-election."

Norm gave Jim a wary look. "The President is being treated badly by the media and the elites. I want to show him that I support him."

Jim smirked. "Did you see that on the news this morning? Oh, wait, the power's out, our cell service is out, and the TV stations around here aren't broadcasting. From what I've read, it's because the President's supporters are blowing up infrastructure and shooting it out with police. Don't tell me you slept through all the shooting and explosions during the night."

Norm reacted with over-the-top anger that made Jim think it was a bit of showmanship. "You're making that up. Nothing but lies. Why would you make up lies like that? Get away from me."

Jim shook his head slowly, "Okay I'll go. I sincerely hope your sign protects your family from whatever is coming. And if the President drives down our dead-end road, I'm sure he'll appreciate your support." Jim continued up the street, re-holstering his gun as he went.

It was a short drive to the highway where, as expected, the stoplights were not working. Jim stopped the car and looked at what was left of the gas station across the highway. That was definitely the source of the explosion during the night. The building was severely damaged, as was the house next door. The station's canopy had collapsed onto the pumps and what looked like a burned-out police car was poking out from under the wreckage. If anyone was in that squad car, they hadn't stood a chance. After looking at the scene for a minute, it hit Jim that not only were there no authorities securing the place, but there was no crime scene tape around the area. It was like the explosion happened and nobody cared. Jim decided against a closer inspection on the off chance that some fuel could still be burning underground.

He took a left onto the highway and headed up toward the mall area. It was less than a mile to the mall and Jim didn't see any other traffic or people along the way. He followed the highway to the left as it swung around past the front of the mall and now he could see that the building had been damaged by fire in one section. He couldn't tell if the fire was still burning, but there were no fire trucks in the parking lot. Making sure there was nobody around him, he pulled off to the side of the road and took a closer look through his binoculars. Scanning carefully, he could see that the glass doors at the main entrance had been shattered and now he noticed a few vehicles parked near that entrance. While he watched, a couple of men came out with their arms full and deposited whatever they were carrying into the trunk of a car. They did a quick scan of the parking lot and then headed back into the mall.

Jim had seen enough. No emergency services here either and brazen looting in daylight. It was safe to assume any protection for him and his family was going to be up to Jim today. He set down the binoculars and headed up the highway driving carefully through the intersections where the stoplights weren't working. A couple miles took him past the Walmart and the RV dealership into Hermantown. It was quiet out there, only a couple of other vehicles passed going the other way on the highway. Other than the traffic signals not working, the highway had the vibe of a really quiet, early weekend morning in the summer. As he got through Hermantown and was nearing Pike Lake, he thought to take his phone out of his pocket and turn it on. Cell service was working here. When he got near the intersection of Highway 53 and Midway Road he was surprised to see the stoplight working. He pulled off to the side of the road to think about this for a minute. Maybe getting out of town today wasn't going to be any problem at all.

As he sat thinking, a car zipped past him, drove through the intersection, and headed up the highway. *Where did they come from?* Jim cursed himself for not checking his mirrors and paying better attention to his surroundings. He watched as the car sped off into the distance, then the driver slammed on the brakes and the car skidded to a stop. Jim grabbed his binoculars to see what was going on and could see that the driver had put the car in reverse and started to back up when bullets started punching through the front of the car. Jim could hear the bursts from what sounded like an automatic weapon and could see the results as the car was taking shot after shot. Eventually the car slowly rolled off the side of the road and hit a tree. Then it stopped.

Jim quickly got moving. He pulled forward and turned off the highway then turned right onto the frontage road where he parallel parked between a couple of cars that were already sitting there. Then he climbed into the back seat of his SUV so he could see over the seat out the back window without being too visible. With his binoculars, he couldn't see the shot-up car from here, but he could see the highway. Within a couple of minutes, a pickup truck came up the road and stopped near where the car had run off the road. Three men were in the bed of the truck wearing body armor over camouflage clothing and holding rifles. Two of the men in the back jumped out, guns pointed towards the car, and started moving that way. The pickup truck turned around in the road and waited. The third man stayed in the back of the truck, peering over the lift gate and looking in Jim's direction. At this distance and without binoculars, Jim didn't think the man could see him. Apparently, the shot-up car still worked because after a few minutes of waiting it drove slowly past the truck and the truck followed it up the highway. Jim wondered what they did with the driver and any passengers that had been in the car. Jim needed to process what he just saw, but sitting here out in the open probably wasn't the best place to do that. He hopped back into the driver's seat, scanned the area carefully, started the car, and headed back towards home.

Jim used the driving time to try to put things together in his mind as best he could. What did he know? *The main highway out of town was currently blocked by armed men ready to shoot without warning. Cell service and power seem like they were operational, at least in some places, further from the center of the city. There are dozens of roads that lead out of the Duluth area, and it's unlikely that they all can be blocked, but all the little highways through the Northern part of Minnesota go through towns and cities of different sizes. How do we pick a route that gets us to the Canadian border? What are the chances there are going to be armed men blocking the roads that lead to the border crossings? Some of those border crossings include bridges that would be pretty easy to defend if the border cities are as lawless as Duluth is right now. Even if we have a caravan of vehicles, full of guns, how can we avoid driving into an ambush?*

Jim pondered these things on the ten-minute drive back to his house. He only encountered a couple of other vehicles on the road as he went. Before he turned onto his street, he pulled his gun back out just in case Norm was up to something, but Norm was nowhere to be seen. He didn't see any other neighbors and he pulled into the driveway without incident. Just to be extra careful, he got out of the car and walked completely around his house looking for any signs that anything was out of the ordinary, but all looked normal. He opened the garage door and parked inside, then closed the door behind him. He unlocked the door to the house and opened it cautiously. "Joy, it's me. I'm back. Is everything okay?"

"We're down the hall packing. The girls aren't too excited about leaving for vacation early."

He walked through the house toward the bedrooms.

"Did you tell them about the campground with a pool?" After a brief pause and at a lower volume, "I'm not sure we can leave today anyway."

She came out of Kelly's room. "What did you see out there?" They headed to the kitchen.

"First, I talked to Chuck's wife."

"LeAnn," Joy interjected.

"Thank you. Names are so hard. Carl told her we were going to Canada and she wants to caravan with us. I told her that would be fine as long as they can help with protection along the way. Then I saw Norm in his yard putting up a campaign sign for the President."

"Really? The election was like a year and a half ago. Did he say why?"

Jim sighed, "To support the President in his time of need. I think Norm knows more than he's willing to let on and he thinks the sign is going to work like the lamb's blood on the doorway during the Passover. He thinks it will protect his family from harm. I can't blame him. I mean, I can blame him for the situation we're in by supporting the candidates he supports, but I can't blame him for trying to ward off the armed mobs now. Wonder if the sign will make him a target for the other side."

"We probably couldn't trust him to be on the right side if something happened in the neighborhood, but his wife has always been nice, and they have kids, so I hope his sign works. What else did you see?"

Jim explained what he saw at the gas station, the mall, and the shoot-out on the highway. "If we do try to go north, we're going to have to find a different way out of town."

He looked at his watch, it was almost 9:30. "How much time do you need to finish packing?"

"My stuff is all packed, I helped Alex get her stuff all packed, Kelly is trying to fit a few more outfits into her suitcase and is deciding what books she wants to bring."

"Okay, so we still need to pack food and medicines, but I can start hauling some stuff out to the RV then. There's one item I need your help with. Can you come downstairs with me?"

She had a quizzical look on her face, "What is it?"

"You know that steel washtub that we used to use as a bathtub for the dog? I want to put that in the RV."

"That tub is huge. Where are you going to put it?"

"If we can fit it through the door, I'm going to put it on the floor between the bench seats of the dinette. If I have to, I'll take the table out to make room. It should fit if I have the measurements right. It may stick out a little past the seats, but it should be fine." He paused and took a deep breath. "Look, it's made out of steel, and I don't know if it will stop a bullet, but the girls should be able to lay down in there, side by side, if we run into trouble. It just might provide enough protection to keep them safe."

She shook her head. "I'll help you carry it out, but you keep making the Canada option sound worse. Let's do it now while the girls are busy in their rooms."

They hauled the heavy washtub out to the RV and it took the two of them working together to maneuver it through the door and wedge it between the bench seats once Jim removed the table. Jim wedged the table between the wall and the tub for some additional protection on that side and hoped they wouldn't need the tub at all.

Jim had come to the decision they should get the RV packed up to go. Even if they didn't leave today, they would be ready to go at a moment's notice. Besides, the food in their refrigerator in the house wasn't going to keep cold anyway, at least the refrigerator in the camper was operational. "Why don't you go back in the house and keep packing. I'll start hauling our stuff into the camper. If we do it efficiently, we might be all packed up by 10:30. Then we'll have to make a final decision."

Joy nodded. "I'll leave the suitcases by the door to the garage. The passports and other documents are in a pouch on the kitchen counter. Are there still a couple of those big plastic totes in the storage area we can fill up with food so you can carry it all in a couple trips?"

"Good thinking. I'll grab them and bring them in the house. We might as well pack as much of the fridge and freezer stuff as we can. It's going to spoil if we don't take it with us."

Jim went to the back storage area of the RV and pulled out a couple of gray, plastic storage totes. He followed Joy through the garage into the house and set them down in the kitchen. "I'm going to open the big garage door and leave all the doors unlocked so I can go back and forth. I'll be watching as much as I can, but yell if someone sneaks past me."

He grabbed a suitcase and headed to the camper. After a number of trips he had loaded all four suitcases in their usual places in the camper, put his laptop bag and backpacks on the floor next to the bed, put the important documents in the sun visor above the passenger seat, and put the girls' backpacks in their usual sitting places for the drive. The solar power station and accessories were stuffed into the rear storage compartment. He was heading back to the house to grab the first tote of food when he saw a vehicle coming up the street. It was a black SUV, and his first thought was that Carl and Julie were coming home, but they should be in Wisconsin by now, so it couldn't be them. He quickly moved behind the camper and unholstered his gun. The SUV stopped at the bottom of his driveway and the passenger window rolled down. Then Julie yelled to him. He put the gun away and walked down the driveway to see why they were back.

Carl got out and came around to talk to him. "We couldn't get to

Wisconsin. We were going to use the Blatnik Bridge, but it looks like a section got blown out and there's no way to drive across it. So we tried the Bong Bridge, but there was a burned-out semi-truck parked across both lanes and the shoulder and there was no way around it. I think the Facebook message you showed me might be true. Looks like you're packing up to head out. Still planning to go to Canada?"

Jim shrugged. "I drove up Highway 53 earlier. A car passed me at Midway Road and didn't get more than another half a mile before it got shot to hell. I didn't see what kind of roadblock they were using, but it was effective. That driver isn't going to see the sunset tonight."

They looked at each other for a few seconds and Jim continued. "I really want to get my family out of here. I think the police are outmanned and outgunned and I don't want to spend another night standing watch, but I also don't want to drive into an ambush and get my family killed. Maybe if we had a tank running point we might stand a chance, but we don't know how many roadblocks we might run into between here and the border."

Carl looked thoughtful for a second. "I don't know anybody with a tank, but I do have something to offer that might swing the odds in our favor a little. We made a stop on our way back and talked to a family friend about wanting to get to the border. He was in Iraq with our son and knows a thing or two about a military convoy. Hopefully he'll be here in a while, and maybe with some friends."

Jim was dumfounded. "Do you really think he could shepherd us safely to the border? That would be my first choice, but I'm worried about my kids. How can a couple of guys, even guys with training, protect us when we don't know what's out there?"

"They'll be here soon. When they get here, we can talk it through. Right now, I need to get our passports and pack some more stuff."

"Got it. Oh, LeAnn asked if she and Chuck could caravan with us. She left to find her daughter who lives in a different part of town, and I haven't seen her since. But they might be joining us."

Carl nodded, "Okay." Then he got in the car and drove up his driveway.

Jim went into the house and started hauling the food items out to the camper. It looked like they were going to be done packing and have some extra time to spare. Once he had stuffed as much food as could fit into the refrigerator and freezer, he dumped out the milk on the lawn and put the extra frozen food into the chest freezer in the garage. The freezer was still cold, but he wasn't sure how long that would last. If they ever got back here, the garage was going to smell awful.

Jim went back in the house. Joy was in the kitchen making a list and crossing things off. "Hey honey, I think we're all packed. Carl is back and wants to go with us. He's asked some veterans that served with his son to help us, so we're going to wait for them. I haven't seen LeAnn or Chuck yet. Everything is quiet outside though."

Joy was looking down at the paper, "I think we packed everything important. Chargers for Alex's CI's, chargers for phones and iPads, they have their pillows and blankets, there's a small tote of books over there that we should bring. Can you think of anything we might have forgotten?"

Jim got his thinking look on his face. "I should grab the car charger. I'm thinking about shutting off the water coming into the house. Oh, and the revolver is still in the bathroom closet. You may need it on the drive." He paused for a second to let that sink in with her. "I'll get the stuff. Let me know if there's anything else you think of. What are the girls doing right now?"

"Kelly is saying goodbye to the stuffed animals in her room that can't come with us and Alex is reading."

He went down the hall and peeked into Alex's room. She was laying on her stomach on her bed deep into a book. He left her alone. Kelly's door was closed so he knocked and waited.

"Yeah, who is it?" Kelly's tone was in the range that normally meant she didn't want to be disturbed.

"It's Dad. Are you going to be ready to go soon?"

There was a loud, resigned sigh from the other side of the door. "I'll be out in a couple minutes."

With Kelly that probably meant that Joy would have to come back and remind her again, but at least he had planted the seed in her mind so she would be ready to go when the time came. He walked through his bedroom and into the bathroom to get the gun and bullets out of the closet. Then he went back out to the garage and grabbed the charger out of the car and put the charger, gun, and box of bullets in the under the dash storage cubby between the driver and passenger seats in the RV. He went back into the garage and looked around for anything else that would be useful. Joy came into the garage and joined him.

"Should we have the girls go wait in the RV? That's what we usually do when we're getting ready to go on vacation."

He shrugged. "I don't know how long it will be before we know whether we're even going to try to leave today. As long as they're staying occupied, I'm fine with waiting." He continued scanning the garage. "I really wish we had some sheets of steel we could put along the walls in the camper for extra protection. For this trip, I'm willing to add as much weight as it takes to our load if it means more safety."

She thought for a few seconds. "What about that big file cabinet in your office? Doesn't it say Steelcase on it? Is that made of steel?"

Jim looked at her slack jawed, "That thing is ancient, but it is made of steel. Between the outer casing and the drawers, there's enough steel to armor up the area around the girls pretty good." He kissed her on the cheek. "There's a reason I married you. I need to take that thing apart quick."

Jim opened the car door and grabbed the crowbar and hammer he had placed on the seat earlier. Then he hurried into the house and up to his office.

Jim pulled out the four drawers of the file cabinet and dumped their contents out of the way on the floor. He was going to make a mess, but that was a problem for future Jim. Once he had the drawers out, he pulled the cabinet to the middle of the room and started prying the connections apart. He wanted to keep the pieces as straight as possible, but time wasn't on his side. He did the best he could and when he was done, he was left with three decent sheets that placed side by side covered about four feet by six feet. Jim hurriedly hauled those pieces out to the front yard, then took a couple more trips to haul out the drawers and the top and bottom pieces of the cabinet.

Jim set the three big pieces down and quickly drilled a couple of holes in each sheet along a straight line near the center of the four by six wall with his cordless drill. From memory he knew the couch he wanted to place the sheet behind was sixty-eight inches long, so he overlapped the sheets a couple inches. He slid a five foot long two by four under the sheets and then bolted the sheets to the wood so they would roughly stay together as one big sheet. He picked up the finished product and decided it would have to suffice for now. If he had more time later, he might put some more work into it. He carried the sheet of steel into the RV and set it behind the couch on the passenger side in the living area. The sheet covered the entire width of the living area wall and from the floor up the three feet of wall and the bottom foot of the window over the couch. If he had time before they left, he would bolt it to the wall, but for now it was just wedged between the wall and the couch.

With the passenger side flank covered, Jim went to work taking apart the drawers. With the eighteen pieces of varying sizes and a bunch of two by four's, he was able to fashion a five foot by four foot sheet to place behind the driver's seat to protect the living room area from the front and a five foot long by one foot wide strip that he bolted to the wall below the dinette window on the driver's side. That would have to do for additional protection because there was nothing left of the file cabinet but the slides for the drawers.

Jim looked at his watch and saw it was closing in on 11:00. He had worked fast, and his work wasn't going to win any awards for quality of construction, but he had gotten it done. Now he wondered if Carl's cavalry was going to show up at all. Keeping himself busy with manual tasks was a great way to keep his mind off the problems ahead of them, but now they were fully packed, he had installed all the protection for the kids he could come up with, and the only thing left to do was try to solve the problem of how to get to Canada alive.

25

July 1 - Outside Calgary - before dinner

Jim was sitting in a camp chair in the shade near the RV when Kelly came bounding out the door. He had been trying to stop his mind from thinking about their current situation by mentally reconstructing a tennis match he had played at a tournament in St. Paul a few years earlier. The match was memorable because Jim had been facing a superior opponent and had combined playing the match of his life with some tactical adjustments to pull off the upset. Thinking through the match, point by point, was a great way to take his mind to a different time and place.

"Hey dad, mom says we're going to have grilled sandwiches and s'mores for dinner. I get to make the campfire, but you have to help me."

Jim stood up. "That sounds good. Why don't you set up the firewood that's over by the fire pit and I'll get the supplies."

Kelly was the family's campfire expert. She took the job very seriously and was a master at keeping a dying fire going by blowing on the embers in just the right place. She began setting up the firewood in the shape that she had determined to be most effective in getting the perfect campfire. Jim went around the side of the camper and opened up the side storage area where they kept their campfire and camp cooking supplies.

He pulled out the heavy bag with the cast iron sandwich cookers and the small tote with the lighter stick, extendable marshmallow cooking sticks, and the fire-starter, kindling items the girls had made from toilet paper rolls in Girl Scouts. By the time he got back around the camper, Kelly had the wood set up to her liking. She grabbed a couple of the fire-starters and set them in the places they would have maximum effect, then asked Jim for the lighter stick. After verifying that Joy had remembered to tie Kelly's hair back, Jim gave Kelly the lighter and supervised as she got the kindling going.

Jim was always impressed with Kelly's ability to get the fire going. He was never a Boy Scout, and his attempts to start campfires when the girls were little always required more attempts than he thought they should. Kelly seemed to just have an innate ability to get it right every time. He looked over at the picnic table. "Did mom say where we're going to eat this meal?"

Kelly was focused on the task at hand and didn't even notice Jim was talking. While keeping a close eye on her, Jim backed over to the camper door and opened it. Without looking inside, he gave a shout. "Hey, honey, should I set up the picnic table?"

Joy was on the top step, less than three feet away, carrying a tote full of food, plates, and napkins. "What?" She said sarcastically, "I can't hear you, you're too far away."

Jim was caught by surprise. "Sorry, didn't think you'd be lurking just inside the door. Are we eating outside? If you can keep an eye on Kelly, I can get the table cover for the picnic table."

"Yes, we're going to eat at the picnic table if we can put it in a shady spot and the bugs don't drive the girls back inside. How long until we can start cooking over the fire?"

Jim shrugged. "Based on prior experience, Kelly will have that thing roaring in about ten minutes. I haven't noticed any bugs, but we could hang the mosquito net from a branch over the table if you're worried."

She smiled. "Check out the big brain on Jim. I'd like to have a relaxing meal without swatting bugs constantly. Do you think the mosquito net would really work out here?"

"Let's see if we can find a shady spot to put the table and then we can figure out if there's a way to hang the net above the table." He looked toward the fire. "Hey Kelly, me and mom need to do a couple of things. Stay a few feet from the fire."

"Okay dad." She was still focused on the task in front of her.

Jim and Joy didn't have to move the table very far to find a spot shaded by a large tree that had a branch about ten feet off the ground that would go roughly over the table. Jim went into the RV and grabbed the mosquito net and the hanging ring. He stood on the table and secured the hanging ring to the tree with some old kite string he kept in his tool kit. Then he hung the mosquito net from the ring, and it draped down to the ground around the table. There was quite a bit of extra netting at the bottom since it was made to cover a king-sized bed with room to spare. He made sure to align the flap on the camper side. Jim thought the kids would end up getting chocolate and marshmallow on the netting during s'mores time, but that they should be able to keep the bugs away from their meal. As long as the kite string held and the whole thing didn't fall on top of them, it was a pretty good set-up. With that step completed, Jim went to get the table covering while Joy and Kelly supervised the fire.

As Jim was putting the table covering on the table, Alex came out of the camper and looked at the unusual set up with a surprised expression. "Why is there a fishing net over the table?"

Kelly had been sitting in a camp chair admiring her handiwork with the fire. She got up and went closer to her sister to make sure Alex could understand her. "It's a mosquito net to keep the bugs away while we eat. Dad, show Alex how to get in."

Jim had completed setting up the table covering and was setting their heavier supplies on the corners of the table covering so it wouldn't blow off the table. He showed Alex where the flap in the netting was located to get in and out of their eating area. "We all need to be careful not to pull too hard on the netting. It's secured to the tree up there, but my knot-tying skills are not Boy Scout level."

Joy finished setting the table with plates, drinks and napkins at every spot.

By now the fire was going full blast. They all filled their sandwich cookers with the ingredients to make the grilled cheese sandwiches of their choosing - bread and cheese for Kelly, bread, cheese, and pasta sauce for Alex and Joy, and bread, cheese, and pepperoni for Jim - and set them up around the fire to cook.

While the sandwiches were cooking, Alex spoke up. "How long has it been since we made campfire sandwiches? I don't remember the last time, it's been so long."

Jim answered first, "I know we made them when we were on Madeline Island. I have the pictures on my phone. That was a fun time taking Windy on a ferry ride across the lake."

Joy jumped in, "I bought the sandwich makers for the trip we took to Monticello and Kitty Hawk. I know we used them somewhere on that trip. I'm pretty sure we used them in Banff when we went to Alaska, too."

Alex had a sad, thoughtful look. "I wish we could go back to Crater Lake. It was so beautiful and tranquil. I was so happy when we were there."

Joy gave her a hug. "That was a great trip. Remember how we played Harry Potter Trivia and dad didn't know any answers?" The girls smiled. "I think we should all share our favorite vacation stories while we eat. I can think of a couple and I'm sure dad could tell vacation stories all night." She paused when Jim's timer went off indicating that the sandwiches should be done. "Okay. I'm going to grab the plates and dad is going to handle the hot sandwich cookers. Time to eat."

Jim dumped the sandwiches onto the plates and Joy handed them out. They all sat down to wait for their food to cool enough to eat.

Kelly spoke up first. "My favorite park is Arches, and my favorite memory is climbing the big rocks when dad couldn't keep up with me. I got to the top and looked back and dad was way down below."

"I was yelling at you to stop and wait for me, but you were so focused on your mission to get to the top," Jim cut in, "and when you finally stopped, I asked you what was on the other side of the rock you were on. Do you remember what you said?"

"I think I said, 'nothing, it just keeps going straight down', and then you told me to crawl towards you very slowly. You were scared I was going to fall off the other side, weren't you?"

Jim nodded, "I was very scared right then. You climbed like a monkey and had no fear back then." He paused for a second. "Mom and I considered getting one of those leashes for kids after that. You were always so quick and impulsive when you were younger."

Joy spoke up, "That's why all the pictures from the Grand Canyon have me holding you girls in a bear hug. They really need more guardrails at that place." She looked over at Alex. "How about you Alex. What was your favorite trip so far?"

Alex thought for a minute. "My favorite National Park is Crater Lake. My favorite part of a trip was when we visited all the places Abraham Lincoln lived and we got to go in his house in Springfield. He moved around a bunch until he found a place where he could be successful. That's what America was all about." She paused for a few seconds. "I also really liked our trip to SeaWorld. Swimming with the beluga whales was neat. My interpreter even got in the pool with us."

Jim and Joy exchanged a look. They both caught that their daughter had referred to the U.S. in the past tense and that was a little concerning. Jim decided to lighten the mood with a story they all knew well.

He pointed at the mosquito net. "Who remembers why mom bought this netting? None of us will ever be able to forget 'The Night of the Mosquitoes'." He paused for effect. "It was June 21st, and we were camped way off the grid in Wrangell-St. Elias National Park. Even though it never got fully dark outside that night, we all went to bed at our normal bedtimes. At about 2 a.m. we all started getting attacked by mosquitoes. Kelly buried herself in her sleeping bag and wrapped the opening shut around her, mom hid under the covers while ordering me to do something, and I got up to see how bad it was. Alex seemed to be sleeping right through it. When I turned on the lights, there were dozens of mosquitoes in the camper with us, so I started killing them with a flyswatter, but quickly realized that every mosquito I got was probably going to be replaced by five new ones coming in.

So, I made the decision to get us out of the woods and find a different place to spend the rest of the night. You girls stayed buried in your sleeping bags and we just buckled you and the bags into your seats. At about 2:30 we started driving out of the park. In our rush, I had forgotten to put all our stuff away and food, plates, cups, and the toaster all went flying off the counter on the first left hand curve. By a little after 3:00 we were back on the main highway. It was light enough to drive without the headlights. By 3:30 we were parked in a pullout on the highway, and I spent half an hour swatting the remaining mosquitoes. By 4:00 we were all back in bed, but the walls in the living area were covered in blood from where all the mosquitoes had been splatted. The place looked like a crime scene. When we got up later that morning, we cleaned up the walls. I still don't know where the mosquitoes got in and we've never experienced anything like it since then. When we got home from our trip, mom went on Amazon and ordered this netting, and this is the first time we've used it."

"That's called deterrence," Joy interjected. "Now that we're ready for a mosquito infestation, we'll never experience another one. It was money well spent."

Joy smiled. "I want to talk about our trip to visit all the parks in Utah. That was the trip where it seemed like every time I tried to take a shower, something bad happened. Do you remember that Jim?"

"I sure do, dear. None of it was your fault though."

"First we were spending the night at a Walmart somewhere in Nebraska or Colorado and even though I turned on the water heater and did everything right, the water in the shower was freezing cold."

Jim nodded. "That was my fault dear. I messed up the little switches on the water pipes between the water heater and the shower. I got it fixed after you let me know it was a problem."

She gave him a look that made it seem all was not yet forgiven on that score. "A couple nights later we were between Canyonlands and Natural Bridges at a little campground that was mostly a parking lot and not two minutes after I turned on the water heater the carbon monoxide detector went off and scared all of us." She looked at Jim. "Of course, you were off talking to the guy who ran the campground, as usual, so the girls and I hurried outside and I sent Kelly to find you."

Jim spoke up again. "It wasn't your fault. It was really windy that evening and the wind blew the propane fumes from the water heater back into the camper. Once we shut off the water heater and opened the windows for a few minutes, everything was fine. The alarm stopped chirping, you still got to take your shower that night, and the water temperature was fine. It was just surprising at the time. That one was nobody's fault, not even mine."

She gave him a fake glare. "Then a few nights later I actually took a shower with hot water and without setting off any alarms, but after I was done the floor in the little hallway next to the shower was covered in water. At that point I told you I was done showering for the rest of the trip."

He squeezed his nose. "Thankfully, I was able to change your mind on that one since we were on the road for a while on that trip after that. The water leak was from some plumbing connections that came loose on that crappy gravel road that led to City of Rocks. I regret pushing through and driving up that road, it probably took a year off the useful life of Windy. Plus, I don't remember what it cost us for repairs at the end of that trip, but it was over $1,000. Another lesson learned the hard way."

Kelly spoke up. "I'm ready for s'mores. Can we have dessert now?"

They all took a break to cook their marshmallows and make their s'mores. Joy broke out the graham crackers and chocolate bars and set them up on plates while Jim handed out the marshmallow cooking sticks. The girls cooked their marshmallows under supervision and Joy helped them get the sticky, melty marshmallows into the cracker sandwiches. Alex liked her s'more without chocolate, so Kelly used an entire Hershey bar on her s'more. While the girls sat down to eat, Joy and Jim cooked their marshmallows then joined the girls.

It was still a beautiful day and the sun was low enough that they had plenty of shade with all the trees surrounding their campsite. Other than the mosquito net looming over them, Jim felt like they were, at that moment, living out a scene from a campground promotional advertisement - smiling family of four, happily devouring s'mores at the picnic table. Kelly had melted chocolate on her chin and sticky marshmallow on her fingers and Alex had a satisfied grin on her face. *After everything we've been through these last four weeks, we've earned this little bit of happiness.*

After dessert, and some clean-up, Joy turned the conversation toward the future. "Girls, tomorrow we're driving to Calgary to meet with someone with Canadian Immigration Services. If everything goes well, they are going to get us set up so we can stay in Canada for a while and maybe help us find a place to live that isn't on wheels until we can go back home. We don't know how long that will be, but for now we're going to make decisions with the expectation we will be here through the school year."

Alex objected, "But we don't know Canadian history. I'm going to fail history."

Jim smiled. "Honey, for this coming year I don't think any of us are going to be very concerned about your grades in a new school in Canada."

"Free pass to skip homework all year. Yes! I'm going to like Canadian school," Kelly whooped.

"We still expect you to make some effort," Joy chided. "It's not a free year of goofing off. We just aren't going to hold you to the same standards as last school year because everything is going to be new and different. We aren't sure where we're going to be able to settle down, but we want it to be a family decision so this evening I want you both to write down any thoughts you have about where you might like to live for a while."

"And it won't be Medicine Hat or Moose Jaw no matter how much you'd like to live in a place with a name like that," Jim deadpanned. "I'm looking at you Kelly, I know you were thinking Medicine Hat."

Kelly smiled. "I want to live in a house with my own bedroom. And can we replace all the stuff I couldn't bring with me?"

Alex spoke up. "My friend from ASL camp lives near Toronto. Maybe that would be a good place to live."

Joy nodded. "That's a place we can consider. After our meeting we'll get together as a family and figure it out. Dad and I will make the final decision, but we want to include your ideas in what we decide. And we will see about a house, but we might end up with an apartment. We'll do our best to get three bedrooms. Now let's get this mess cleaned up so dad can go hang out with his new friend. If you two can agree on a movie, you can have some extra screen time."

26

∽

June 6 - Duluth - around 11 a.m.

Jim went into the RV and pulled out a Minnesota map from the drawer by the bed. He scanned the top of the state for roads that crossed into Canada. From what he could see, there were seven border crossings. He had used three of them on previous trips over the border and all of those crossings had bridges. Jim thought those crossings might be risky today based on Carl's report on the status of the bridges to Wisconsin, so he concentrated on the four crossings west of Lake of the Woods. They would have to drive through a lot of Northern Minnesota to get to any of those crossings. That drive would be on small two-lane highways that went through lots of little towns and some bigger towns. The crossing north of Warroad was the closest. He pulled out his phone and connected to the Wi-Fi. According to his mapping app, it was a four-and-a-half-hour drive to Warroad.

Jim opened up his browser and searched "Canada border services agency." A couple of clicks got him to the page with current wait times for border crossings. Fort Frances and Rainy River were listed as closed, just as he suspected they might be. It appeared that the other crossings between Minnesota and Manitoba were open right now. He found a phone number for Border Information Services and took a screenshot of it for later.

As he was pondering what to do next, he saw out the window that a couple of vehicles were coming down the street. A large black pickup truck was followed by a blue Jeep Wrangler with the top off. From what he could see, the Jeep had two men inside dressed in what looked like combat fatigues. He hoped they were the cavalry, because if they were the other team there was likely to be some carnage in the next few minutes and he didn't like his chances.

The truck swung around the cul-de-sac and stopped in front of Carl's house. Two men got out, both wearing military garb and body armor. They each had a gun strapped to their thigh. The Jeep stopped on the other side of the cul-de-sac, in front of Jim's house and two men similarly dressed got out.

Jim stayed in the camper until he saw Carl come down his driveway to greet the newcomers, then he stuffed the Minnesota map in his pocket and exited the camper slowly with his hands held over his head. "I'm with Carl, not a threat," he shouted.

Carl introduced Jack, the driver of the pickup truck, as a member of the same platoon as his son in Iraq. Jack introduced his team. Steve was riding in the truck, RJ was driving the Jeep, and Quinn was the passenger in the Jeep. They were all veterans of Iraq and Afghanistan and looked fit enough to deploy again immediately.

Jack took the lead. "Okay, you two want to get to Canada and we're here to help you get there." He looked at Jim while pointing at the RV. "Is that the vehicle you intend to drive?"

Jim nodded. "Yeah. Me, my wife, and my two daughters. I installed some steel sheeting inside the living area for protection, but I'm not going to be very fast or agile."

Jack shook his head. "Safe to say we're not going to outrun anybody. Is this everybody that's coming?"

"Not yet." Carl spoke up. "We have another family that should be joining us soon. Right there." He pointed up the street. "Looks like they're finishing packing up their car."

Jim pulled out his map and spread it on the hood of the Jeep. "If you don't mind me speaking first, I'll tell you what I know that might help with your decision-making. There are seven border crossings in Minnesota. Three of them are currently closed." He pointed to the one along Lake Superior, International Falls-Fort Frances, and Rainy River. "The four to the west of Lake of the Woods are open according to the website as of about five minutes ago. This one is closest, just north of Warroad. It's about five hours away on a normal day. Based on what I've seen and what Carl's seen, I would bet the road to the border station is going to be blocked in some way and we may have to fight our way through it."

Carl nodded, "If it's anything like the bridges to Wisconsin, the road will be blocked. And if it's blocked by people with guns like Jim saw up the highway, it's not going to be easy to get past them."

While they were talking, Joy and the girls came out and stood in the driveway next to the door to the RV. Joy wanted to know what they were planning but didn't want the girls to get too close where they might hear too much.

Jack turned to Jim, "Show me where the highway was blocked off."

Jim pointed at the map to the spot where the roadblock was. "There's a frontage road alongside the highway there, but I didn't check to see if it was clear. I didn't want to take that risk by myself."

Chuck and LeAnn walked up to where they were standing. "Sorry we're so late," LeAnn said, "I couldn't convince Jennifer to come with us without her boyfriend. You know how twenty-five-year-old girls are about their boyfriends. She went off looking for him. I'm praying she gets here before you need us to leave."

Just then Chuck looked up the street and said, "Here comes Norm, is he coming with us?"

Norm was walking up the middle of the street with a rifle. The muzzle was pointed down and to the side, but Norm had a very serious look on his face, something between anger and hate from what Jim could determine. Carl stepped away and started walking towards Norm with his hands out in front of him, palms out to show he wasn't threatening. Carl and Norm had spent many hours chatting in the street over the years and had always gotten along well.

"What are those militia guys doing here?" Norm yelled. "They need to get out of this neighborhood now."

Carl stopped halfway between Norm and the group, "Look Norm, these guys served with my son. They're the good guys. They're here to help us get out of town. We're going to be leaving in a few minutes and you'll probably never see these guys again. Nobody is here to start any trouble."

Norm looked at Carl like he just now recognized who he was. "Carl? What are you doing here? This morning you said you were going to your cabin in Wisconsin." Norm's anger seemed to be turning to disorientation.

"We couldn't get there. The Blatnik Bridge has been blown up and the Bong Bridge is blocked by burning vehicles. Highway 53 has a roadblock manned by an armed militia shooting anyone who tries to leave town. We're just figuring out a plan and then we're going to leave."

Norm's attitude flipped again. "Bullshit!" He fumed. "That's the same crap Jim tried to feed me this morning. You guys are up to something and I'm not going to let you intimidate my family." He adjusted his grip on the gun and held it in front of him menacingly. "You've got ten minutes then I'm coming back to make you leave." As he started to move away, he added, "I can't believe you've become a traitor like this Carl. I always suspected Jim, but not you."

As Norm was backing away, Steve, who had been standing near the front of Jack's truck and away from the rest of the group, took a step towards the truck. The movement startled Norm and he swung his AR-15 up and fired off a burst at Steve. Steve was hit twice in his right leg. Before any of the civilians had recovered from the shock of the gunfire, Jack, RJ, and Quinn put at least six shots into Norm and he was dead before his body hit the ground. Jim hadn't even had time to unholster his gun.

Carl, who dropped to the ground at the first sound of Norm's shots, screamed, "What the hell Norm!" Then he looked back and could see that Norm was beyond criticism.

Jim hurried over to where Norm had fallen to check if he had a pulse. When it was clear Norm was gone, he carefully picked up the rifle and headed back towards the Jeep. He looked over at Joy and the girls and saw that Joy had squatted down and had one arm wrapped around each of their daughters, pulling them in tightly to her sides to shield them from the gunfire, but they were still standing motionless, shocked by what just happened.

RJ and Quinn hurried over to where Steve was lying on the ground. As they were assessing his wounds, a shot rang out and the bullet pinged off the fire hydrant in the center of the cul-de-sac, not ten feet from them. They quickly pulled Steve behind the truck and everyone ducked for cover behind the vehicles. The shot had come from up the street well beyond where Norm's body was lying in the road.

Jim ran over to his family where Kelly was just staring at Norm's bloody body, she seemed to be in some sort of shock. "Caleb's dad got shot……he's dead," her voice was almost robotic and had an unusually high pitch.

Alex was looking warily at the rifle Jim was carrying. Jim set it down carefully and helped Joy herd his family into the RV. He helped the girls into the washtub and told them they needed to lie down for a little while and stay flat. Joy ducked down beside the tub where she also had cover and could talk to the girls and reassure them. Jim could hear sporadic shots coming from up the street hitting the Jeep and the neighbor's mailbox. The shooter seemed to be taking his time between shots, either to conserve ammunition or waiting for a target to come out from behind cover.

Jim grabbed his binoculars off the couch in the camper and headed out the door. He picked up Norm's rifle and strapped it over his shoulder then went around to the back of the RV and climbed the ladder to the roof. When he got near the top, he put the binoculars to his eyes and then peered as carefully as he could over the top of the roof to see if he could spot the shooter. From this height he could see over Nancy's privacy fence. He scanned the tree line of the empty lot half a block up the street on the other side. When he finally saw the shooter lying on the ground behind a tree, he noticed that the shooter's rifle was pointed right at him. A shot rang out and the satellite internet dish shattered onto the roof of the RV. Jim quickly got his head below roof level and climbed down as fast as he could. Nancy's fence was just long enough to shield him from the shooter's view at ground level while he was standing at the back of the RV. He waved to the rest of the group and pantomimed that he saw the shooter lying on the ground across the road and he was going to go around the back of the houses to try to get a good shot. Jack signaled that he understood.

Jim worked his way around Nancy's fence and then sidled along the back of her house. At the far corner he peered around, but Chuck's house blocked his view of the shooter's location. He quickly moved between the houses and through Chuck's back yard. At the corner of Chuck's house, he got Norm's rifle ready. He knew nothing about how the gun worked so he hoped the safety was still off. He figured it would take him a couple seconds after leaning around the corner to find the shooter and start firing. He hoped the shooter wasn't waiting for him to pop out right here. He raised the rifle and leaned around the corner of the house. The shooter hadn't moved so Jim spotted him quickly, but when Jim pulled the trigger, the gun was in full automatic mode. It just started spraying bullets and Jim lost control of the muzzle without hitting his target. He didn't know how many shots he fired, but they all hit trees and air. Cursing at himself, he quickly backtracked as the shooter fired a couple of shots that hit the corner of Chuck's house.

Jim hustled through Chuck's back yard and was going to come around the house on the other side when he heard what sounded like a swarm of bugs. He listened more closely and realized it was a small drone. He was carefully working his way along the side of Chuck's house when he heard a small explosion accompanied by a scream. He waited a few seconds just listening. Now he could still hear the drone, but it was fading and there were groans from across the street. He peeked quickly around the corner of the house and could see the shooter was down, curled up in the fetal position with his rifle sitting untouched nearby. Jim watched for a few seconds then tried to mimic what he'd seen in war movies. Holding Norm's rifle at his shoulder, aimed at the shooter, he moved as quickly as he could down the driveway, across the road, and up to where the shooter was curled up. When he got there, he kicked the shooter's gun away and then took a good look at him. It was Norm's sixteen-year-old son, Caleb, and he was badly wounded.

"NOOOO!" Jim screamed frustration. "WHY??!!!"

Jim stood over the boy, seething, and sobbing. Eventually Carl slowly walked up. "Is it Norm's boy?"

Jim nodded slowly. "He's gone. Fuck."

Carl picked up Caleb's rifle. "He was a good kid. It shouldn't have come to this. I don't know how his mom is going to make it through this. We need to go before she comes out with a bazooka and gets payback on all of us."

As they hustled back to the rest of the group Jim asked, "Was that a grenade dropped by a drone?"

Carl nodded. "These guys have tools and skills you've never even dreamed of. If anybody can get us to the border, Jack can do it."

As they got to Norm's body, Chuck met them and the three of them carried him out of the road and set him on the grass. Chuck said a few words and made the sign of the cross.

Jack and his crew were evaluating Steve's injuries. They had some bandages in the truck, and they patched him up as well as they could quickly, but he wasn't going to be doing any military maneuvers on that right leg for quite a while.

Jack turned to Carl. "Steve is going to have to stay here. Can we put him up in your place until we get back? He's going to bleed on your furniture a bit."

Steve cut him off, "I can just stay in the garage with the door open. There's a clear line of sight from there all the way up the street. Leave me my sniper rifle along with my other equipment and I'll be able to protect myself."

Julie spoke up. "You can take the garage or the house, whichever you want. We can put some blankets on the floor that you can use to make it more comfortable in the garage." Looking around. "Does anybody have an old mattress or couch cushions?"

Jim responded. "I've got an old couch in my basement and we can grab the cushions off of that. If someone wants to help me, there's a wheelchair and crutches in my garage that Steve can use, from after Alex had those operations on her legs."

Carl nodded. "Let's go."

They hurried over to Jim's house and Carl wheeled the chair with the crutches in it over to where Steve was lying on the ground. Jim went back into the basement and grabbed the cushions off the old couch and hurried back to Carl's garage. He stopped on the way to let Joy and the girls know that the shooting was done, but they should stay in the camper for now. They could try using their devices, but the Wi-Fi probably wasn't going to work. *That satellite dish was the best money I ever spent. It probably saved my life.*

They had to adjust the crutches since Steve was quite a bit taller than Alex, but he was able to use them to get up the driveway. Jim showed him how the leg supports attached to the wheelchair and how he could adjust their height. Steve sat down in the chair and they helped him get his right leg elevated, then he practiced wheeling around a little to get a feel for it. "If I have to move, I'm ditching this thing for the crutches."

Julie set up the cushions and some blankets along the wall while RJ and Quinn brought all of Steve's equipment out of the truck and set it up where he could reach it. Carl pointed out the refrigerator at the back of the garage. "There's all kinds of soft drinks and some beer in there. It probably isn't cold anymore, but you'll have plenty to drink for a few days. You can eat any of the food in there since it won't be good much longer."

Jim spoke up, "Yeah, there's a freezer in my garage that's full of food. You can have all of it. There's a fire pit on my patio behind the garage and a bin full of firewood so you can cook any of the meat from the freezer. Hopefully you won't be stuck here that long, but take anything out of my garage if it helps you."

While they were setting Steve up in Carl's garage, Chuck and LeAnn got their car and pulled it up behind the Jeep. Their daughter Jennifer and her boyfriend Paul pulled up behind them in a 1980's era red Corvette that had seen better days.

Jack, RJ, and Quinn spent some time alone with Steve and then came down the driveway together. Jack took charge. "Okay, we are going to do a convoy out of this neighborhood and we're going to rendezvous here." He pointed at a spot on the map that was a couple miles short of the roadblock Jim encountered earlier. "I'm going to lead and I need someone to ride shotgun." He looked around and pointed at Chuck. "Can you handle the AR-15 that guy used to shoot Steve?"

Chuck nodded.

"Okay, you're with me. Carl, you and Julie follow me. Are you all riding together?" He pointed at Leann, Jennifer, and Paul.

Paul spoke first. "No, we need two cars when we get there."

Jack's eyes narrowed, "Can that thing really make it to Canada?" He pointed at the Corvette.

"She's stronger than she looks, sir." Paul had a little sarcasm in his voice.

Jack let it go. "Okay, gray car follows Carl, red Corvette after the gray car, RV behind the Corvette, and RJ and Quinn will take up the rear. We are going to maintain a following distance of no closer than 100 yards, but not so far that you lose touch with the vehicle in front of you. Understood?"

Everyone nodded in agreement.

LeAnn pulled Jennifer aside, "You need to ride with me since your dad is riding up front with Jack. Paul can handle himself. I need you by my side."

Jim caught up with Jack. "Hey, I don't want to add any more to the degree of difficulty we're facing here, but I just about got shot a few minutes ago and want you to be aware that if something happens to me, my wife is blind so she's not going to be able to just take my spot and drive the RV. I know it's a lot to ask, but can you make sure someone keeps my family on the road if I go down before we get to Canada?"

Jack looked noncommittal. "I'll let the guys know."

Jim went back to the RV and climbed into the driver's seat. "Okay ladies, we're heading to Canada. Everybody take your usual spot for now, but if I say to take cover you girls need to lay down in that tub immediately. Understand?"

"I'm going to ride back here with the girls," Joy declared. "If you don't need me up front, I think we'll all feel better having me close by."

Jim nodded. "Agreed. If you need to take cover, your spot is on the floor between the tub and the couch. That will have the most protection from the remains of my file cabinet."

Jim started the engine and waited as the other vehicles moved out of the way of his driveway, then he worked his way into his spot in the caravan. For the second time today, he said a silent prayer for the safety of his family, and he prayed for forgiveness for his part in the deaths that had taken place and what might still be in store for them. As they drove past Norm's house he added a prayer for Norm's wife and daughter and the suffering they were going to experience once they found out what happened on the street today.

27

∽

July 1 - Outside Calgary - early evening

Kelly helped Jim make sure the fire was completely out, she was a stickler for fire safety. He took down the mosquito netting and packed it in one of the storage compartments – now that it had been used outside it would have to be washed before Joy would allow it back in the bedroom of the camper.

The girls were able to agree on a movie pretty quickly once the dinner mess was cleaned up. They sat down in their places and Joy started the DVD.

Jim and Joy went to the bedroom for a quick chat.

Jim started, "I told Chad I would come over this evening and give him some details of our drive to Canada. It might be a long conversation. Can you dig out all of our important documents so we're ready for our meeting tomorrow?"

"That won't take long. They're all in that zippered pouch in the drawer. Are you sure you want to relive that day to a guy you just met? That might not be healthy for you and why share something so personal with a stranger?"

Jim took her hands, "I think he's a good guy and he says he's thinking about sneaking back into the U.S. before winter to see if he can help the good guys. He got out before anything happened and it could help him to know what we saw. It's been over three weeks since we left and who knows how much has changed in that time, but I can at least give him an accurate account of what it was like back then. I don't think there's any harm in sharing and it might be therapeutic for me, but you're the psychology major, not me."

She sighed, "Yeah, fine. You know I worry about things. Go ahead. We're leaving here in the morning and you'll probably never see your new friend again."

He leaned in and gave her a kiss. "Thanks babe. I'll lock the door on my way out. If the girls want to stay up late tonight, it's a holiday and you could give them a pass. I won't even drag everyone out of bed at seven tomorrow, like I normally do on vacation."

"Just don't stay out too late. Bedtime is always Kelly's worst time these days."

"Understood. I will try to be conscious of the time. I'll see you later."

Jim hurried out past the girls as quietly as possible so he wouldn't disturb their movie time. He grabbed a couple bottles of water on his way out the door. It was still light out and Jim wondered if he would interrupt Chad's dinner time. They hadn't agreed on a specific time, so he figured he didn't need to stand on ceremony. He walked across the road and up the driveway to Chad's camp site.

Chad came out of his camper as Jim approached and greeted him. "Hey Jim, I was wondering when you were going to stop by. I looked across the way a while ago and you had some crazy tent set up over your picnic table. What was up with that?"

Jim smiled. "My kids really don't like bugs. The only way we could get them to eat outside was to drape a mosquito net over the table. First time I've tried it, but it worked really well."

Chad had a quizzical look on his face. "You travel to a lot of countries where malaria is a problem? I don't think I've ever seen someone use a mosquito net except in movies."

Jim chuckled and told Chad the story of the "Night of the Mosquitoes."

"Alaska, huh. Mosquitoes wouldn't be near the top of my list of things to prepare for when camping in the Alaskan wilderness. Good to know if I ever go up there."

"Glad to help. We've camped in forty-nine states and most parts of Canada. If you need a tip about a location, I may have been there."

Chad looked thoughtful. "Okay, I'll try you. Where have you camped in Oregon? Any place good?"

Jim thought for a minute. "We've spent six or seven nights in Oregon over the years. The best place we stayed I think was called the Southern Oregon RV Park, something like that. Concrete parking pads, full hookups, great Wi-Fi. It was brand new the summer we were there so the tree cover was a little sparse. We spent two nights there it was so nice, and inexpensive. We stayed at a couple of KOA's along I-5 that were okay, nothing to write home about. One of them had a pool the kids liked. There was a place we stayed at in our old RV, I think it was in Woodburn. It was full of brand new class A's, a really fancy place, and we pulled in driving our twenty-year-old class C with the stickers peeling off. I couldn't believe they let us stay there. Probably got lots of complaints from the neighboring campers. The last one was a KOA on Lemolo Lake, near Crater Lake. I can't tell you much about the place because we pulled in around 10 p.m. after driving through wildfires all evening and the whole area was covered in a haze of smoke all night. In the morning we got up and drove straight to Crater Lake without spending any time exploring the campground." He paused. "Okay now that I've talked it through, none of those places are a must see. One of the reasons we installed solar panels on our RV was to limit the number of nights we needed to spend at campgrounds. The plan was to only pay for a night when we needed to fill up the water tank and dump the other tanks."

"Yeah, you haven't sold me on any of those places. Are you ready to talk about how you got to Canada? If you are, I'm ready to listen."

Jim nodded, "Like I said, this is going to take me a while, so get comfortable." After a brief pause to figure out where to start. "The power went out at my house around 1 a.m."

Jim explained everything that happened to him between 1 a.m. and when the caravan of vehicles left the neighborhood.

Chad stopped him at that point, "What do you think happened to your neighbor that set him off like that? Was he always on edge?"

Jim shook his head. "Norm and I probably wouldn't have agreed on much politically, but we never discussed politics. He seemed like a pretty normal guy with a couple kids who I would see out washing his minivan or cutting his grass. There were no signals that would have suggested he thought I was a subversive or that he was paranoid about any of the rest of the neighbors. Every interaction we had before that day was neighborly. He wouldn't have invited me to dinner at his house and I wouldn't have invited him to hang out and watch a football game at my house, but mostly because we both knew we didn't really have much in common. He was the only person on our street who put out political signs every single election, but that was his right and, as far as I know, nobody ever gave him a hard time about it."

"Okay, sorry, didn't mean to stop your momentum. Keep going."

Jim nodded, "So we headed out of the neighborhood and turned onto the highway. We kept our following distances as we drove the same route I had driven earlier that day past the mall and out of town."

28

June 6 - Duluth - about 11:45

Jim kept his distance behind the Corvette as they drove through Hermantown past the Walmart and the RV dealership. There were more cars on the road now and Jim watched them closely as they passed, hoping nobody with bad intentions was in one of them and hoping the guys in the Jeep were covering him. He leaned back in his seat and yelled, "Hey honey, I'd feel better if you all took cover right now. There's a lot of other vehicles out here and I don't know if someone might take a shot at us."

Joy found a couple of blankets to line the inside of the washtub and cushion it for the girls. If they were going to be stuck in there for hours, it should be at least a little bit more comfortable. She helped the girls get in and handed them their iPads. Joy stayed on the couch, laying down to keep herself below the top of the steel plating behind her. "I'm going to buckle the seatbelts across the top of the tub so the girls don't go flying out of there if you have to stop suddenly or something else happens."

"Good thinking. I'll do my best to drive safely."

The red Corvette was swerving from lane to lane in front of them and Jim wondered what was going on with that young man driving the car. They hadn't been on the road ten minutes and he was already driving erratically. The Corvette started to accelerate and pull away from Jim. Jim held back because he could see LeAnn's car not much farther ahead.

Paul kept speeding until he pulled even with LeAnn, then he drove side by side with her for a while before slamming on his brakes then quickly hitting the gas again so that he fell in right behind LeAnn. Either Paul was not capable of following directions, or he was not taking very seriously the situation they were in. Either way, Jim worried that Paul was going to be a problem for them at some point in this operation. He checked his mirrors and saw that the Jeep was still following behind him. He felt like his position in the convoy right now was probably the safest his family could have hoped for with trained soldiers covering their rear, but the motorhome felt like a really big target now that they were out in the open.

A little over a mile from the roadblock Jim had encountered that morning, Jack turned into a parking lot and the convoy followed him. When Jim turned into the entrance, Jack was standing by his truck waiting to give him instructions. Jim noted that the lot they were in was a used car lot. He rolled down his window to hear what Jack had to say.

Jack leaned in, "Find a place to park so it looks like your camper is just another used vehicle for sale. I'm going with RJ and Quinn to see if we can find a way past that roadblock ahead. From what you said it's just past the last stoplight, right?" Jim nodded. "Okay. Wait here until we get back. Try to stay out of sight, but protect yourselves if you need to."

Jim gave a thumbs-up then pulled forward and drove past the first two rows of cars and found a place to park where he could point the RV toward the road and there was plenty of room on both sides that someone would have to cross to get to the camper. Once he was parked, he watched as Jack grabbed a duffle bag out of his truck, put it in the Jeep, hopped into the Jeep with RJ and Quinn, and the three of them headed up the highway. Jim pulled out his phone and started a timer. He wasn't sure how long to give them before he should be concerned, but he didn't want to lose track of how long they were gone. After setting the timer, he noticed there was cell service here.

Turning back to Joy, "Hey honey, if I dial the number for the Canadian Border Services can you sit on hold and then find out if there are any crossings open between Minnesota and Canada if someone answers?"

"We have cell service here?" She was surprised. "Can you turn on your hot spot so we can use our iPads while we're here?"

"Yep. But give me your phone first so I can dial this number."

She pulled out her phone, "Just tell me the number. Do you really think I'll get through?"

"The website said it might take up to thirty minutes to get a representative, so plan for it to take a while, but something has to go right for us today. The universe owes us." He read off the number.

"And what do I need to find out?"

He grabbed the small notebook they kept in the front of the RV to write down to-do lists as they travelled, and handed it back to her. "Find out which border crossings are open today between Minnesota and Ontario or Manitoba and the hours. Even if things go great, we probably aren't going to get to any of them before this evening."

He turned back to his phone and turned on the hot spot. "Hey girls, you should be able to use my hot spot if you want to now. If you want to sit up for a while you can. Does anybody want some water?"

Joy grabbed four bottles of water and handed them out. She had her phone to her ear. The girls sat up on either side of the tub. It made Jim think of when they were little and took baths together, sitting facing each other at opposite ends of the bathtub. Jim turned back to scan the highway and the lot in front of them. Jack's truck had been left in the row closest to the road. Chuck and LeAnn were in their car – they were parked on the end of the second row. Carl parked his SUV right by Jack's truck. Jennifer joined Paul in his car, and he parked right next to the sales office. Jim checked his timer, but it had only been five minutes.

The time sitting in the used car lot seemed to drag on forever to Jim. He scanned the front, then the driver's side, then the mirror on the driver's side, then the screen showing the view from the backup camera, then the passenger side mirror, then out the passenger side window. Repeat. Repeat. Repeat. Kelly asked for a book and Joy found it for her. Kelly asked for her headphones and Joy found them for her. Joy sat with the phone to her ear while looking at her iPad.

There was a little traffic on the highway, mostly going towards Duluth, but it was just a handful of vehicles. On a normal day this highway would be quite busy with hundreds of vehicles passing in the time they had been sitting there. Jim wondered what percentage of the local population knew the roads out of town were a deadly hazard. It had to be more than just their group. And the people who were making the roads deadly, of course - how many of them were out there?

Joy started talking and it startled Jim. "Hello, hi, yes, I'm calling to find out what border crossings are open between Canada and Minnesota and what time they close today. Can you provide me with that information?" There was a long pause, then Joy started writing on the notepad. She kept saying, "uh-huh" and "OK" and "yes" for a while. Then she thanked the person and the call ended.

Looking down at her notes. "So the crossings that are open are all between Minnesota and Manitoba. Sprague is open until 6:00, Piney is open until 10:00, Tolstoi is open until 10:00, and Roseau-South Junction is open until 8:00. He said he didn't know if we'd be able to get to the border crossings, though. His reports say the roads on the American side are impassible right now, but the reports didn't specify what made them impassible. He also said to expect a larger than normal military presence at any border station if we do get there."

"That's pretty much what we expected. We have to hope it's just the roads that are blocked and they haven't taken over the U.S. Border stations. If they have the American border stations, it's going to be hard to get the RV past them – if we get that far. It's probably too much to hope that the Canadians would come across the border to help us if we got pinned down trying to escape, but it's nice to know they're protecting their border from armed invaders."

Jim continued scanning their surroundings. The wait was seeming interminable when he finally spotted the Jeep on the other side of the highway. It drove through the grassy median and pulled into the parking lot. Jim noticed that RJ was driving and Jack was in the passenger seat, but Quinn wasn't with them. Jack got out and signaled for the group to gather around him. RJ scanned the road while the drivers and Chuck listened to Jack.

"The road is open for now. Quinn's up there making sure it stays open until we get through, so we need to move quickly. Same formation. You'll have to drive on the left shoulder at the roadblock, but there's plenty of space, even for the RV. Once we're on the open highway we're going to vary speeds based on what I'm seeing up front so pay attention to your following distances. Okay, move out."

Jim approached Jack and relayed the information from Joy's call to Border Services. "Don't know if that changes your planned route, but that's what we know," he added.

Jack shrugged, "Right now we need to get past that roadblock and get Quinn. We can stop further north and plan the route once we put this area behind us. Let's go."

Jim hurried back to the RV and fell into line behind the Corvette. Jack set a fast pace through the intersection where Jim had stopped this morning and up the highway. He slowed considerably as he approached the roadblock and steered onto the shoulder to get around it. Jack didn't linger once he got past the roadblock, he sped up and kept going. Jim watched the cars in front of him work their way through the roadblock, which consisted of at least five burned-out cars lined up across the highway. He noted that the car he saw get shot up that morning was now a part of the blockade. The truck from this morning was parked behind the burned-out cars and it had taken some damage since this morning – probably from Jack and his gang. There wasn't quite enough shoulder room for the RV, so Jim had to put the driver's side wheels on the grass as he passed the obstruction. Just before he swerved out, he checked his mirrors and saw that the Jeep had stopped a couple hundred yards back and Quinn was jumping into the passenger seat. He had been in the trees keeping watch.

Jim slowed way down since half of his wheels were off the pavement. He was just pulling back onto the roadway when he heard a couple of loud pings behind him. Joy screamed. Her scream caused the girls to scream. Jim turned to check on them, but Joy started shouting, "They're shooting at us, get us out of here!"

Jim turned back to the road and floored it. The RV was not made for quick acceleration, but he got it on the road and got it moving. "Is anyone shot? Please tell me you're all okay."

Joy was helping the girls to lay back down in the tub. Kelly was screaming and Alex looked shocked. Joy reassured Jim, "We're okay. I think the steel file cabinet wall stopped them. Sounded like they hit somewhere in front of me, but that really freaked me out. I'm shaking with adrenaline right now."

Jim heard a whole lot more shooting after the two shots that hit the RV, and when he checked the mirrors, he saw that RJ and Quinn were out of the Jeep with their rifles pointed at the trees beyond the roadblock. He hoped they got the shooter and would get back into the formation soon. The idea of being exposed without his rear-guard protection was uncomfortable. "C'mon guys, wrap it up and get back in the Jeep." He was talking to himself as he watched his protectors fade from view behind them. "We need you up here."

Once the girls were tucked back into the tub and Joy had strapped some seatbelts over it, she looked over the back of the couch at the sheet of file cabinet parts and felt around carefully until she found a couple of dents. "Wow, this thing really did stop those bullets." She kneeled on the couch so she could reach down over the sheet of metal. "There's a couple of holes in the wall here about a foot below the window. What are we doing Jim? We're barely out of Duluth and we already have two bullet holes in the camper. How many more are we going to have by the time we get to the border?"

"We also had our satellite dish shot off. But we've patched things up with duct tape before. We can do the same thing with those holes until we have time to get it fixed right. As long as those guys in the Jeep get back behind us soon, I think we have a really good chance of making it out of this." Jim wasn't sure he completely believed what he was saying, but they didn't really have any other options but to keep going forward.

She looked concerned. "What happened to RJ and Quinn? I thought they were covering us from behind. Where did they go?"

"They stayed behind to get the guy who shot at us and they haven't caught up yet. I'm keeping an eye on the mirrors. I'll let you know when they get back here. So far there hasn't been any other traffic on the high-way. Are the girls okay back there?"

Joy moved closer to Jim and spoke quietly. "They're scared to death right now. How long do you think it will take before we're someplace safe? This is turning out to be a stressful day for them. They saw a man they knew die right in front of them and now they're hiding because people are shooting at us. It's going to take me a long time to recover from this. I don't even want to think about what it's doing to them right now."

"I hear you." He sighed. "Best case, we're on the road for another six hours or so and only have to deal with one more tight situation right before the border. More realistically, we have to weave our way through rural Northern Minnesota and get to the border station that closes at 10:00 right before it shuts down for the night."

She groaned, "I was afraid you were going to say something like that. I'll talk to the girls. We can do it, but they're going to be in rough shape if that's how this day goes."

She moved back and checked in with Alex and Kelly. Jim was focused on keeping the red Corvette in his sight up ahead and watching the rear-view mirror while silently encouraging RJ and Quinn to get back into formation. They had picked up their pace and were doing between 60 and 65 mph most of the time now. Jim wished they would slow down a bit, just until the Jeep caught up.

They had just passed through Cotton when Jim noticed a Minnesota State Patrol vehicle parked in a turnout in the median up ahead. As he passed the squad car, he noted that there was someone in the driver's seat. The car was sitting there like the trooper was running a speed trap and Jim thought there were more important things the state police could be doing today than writing speeding tickets. He instinctively checked his mirror after they passed, but the squad car hadn't moved. They drove a few more miles before Jim saw the flashing lights when he checked his mirror. The squad car was coming up behind him fast. His first instinct was to check his speedometer. He was going 63 in a 65-mph zone, so he wasn't speeding. For now, he decided to ignore the flashing lights and hope the squad car went right by him. It was still moving way faster than him, so that was possible. He undid the strap on his holster and flicked off the safety just in case. Hopefully the trooper was too far away to see that movement in Jim's mirror, and if it wasn't really a trooper, he was going to be ready.

The squad car caught up to the RV quickly and started straddling the lanes not far behind the camper. The driver made his siren squawk a couple times to get Jim's attention. Joy jumped a little. "What was that? Was it a siren?"

"Someone driving a state patrol car is trying to get us to pull over. Stay down. I'm going to slow down a little, but I'm not going to stop."

"You don't think it's really a state trooper? Who else would have a state patrol car?"

Jim slowed down to about 45. "We weren't speeding and don't you think law enforcement has bigger fish to fry today than speeders? I'm going to try to get him to pull up next to us so I can get a good look at the driver. I'm ready to shoot if he has a weapon out."

Jim rolled down the driver's side window, stuck his left arm out, and motioned for the trooper to pull forward. Then he grabbed the wheel with his left hand and pulled out the gun with his right and held it just below the window.

The trooper stayed behind and off to the side of the RV for a minute or so and then swerved behind the camper quickly. The squad car was now too close to see in the mirrors, so Jim looked at the screen for the backup camera and saw the trooper was still following tightly behind him. Suddenly, Jim saw another vehicle out of the corner of his eye and saw that Jack's truck was in the left lane just up ahead moving very slowly. The RV and the squad car passed Jack, who then fell in right behind the squad car and sped up to keep pace. Jim checked his mirror and saw that Chuck was leaning out the passenger window of the truck and had a handgun pointed at the squad car. Just then the Jeep came roaring up behind them and pulled up even with Jack's truck behind the squad car. The driver of the squad car rolled down his driver's side window and started shooting wildly at the Jeep which slowed down to avoid the bullets. Chuck took a few shots at the squad car, one of them pinging off the bumper of the RV and another going through the door to the RV's rear storage compartment. Then Jack slowed down a bit to give Quinn a clear shot and Quinn shot out the front tire of the squad car. The driver lost control of the car and it spun out, off the shoulder and into the grass. As soon as the squad car stopped moving, but before the driver could recover, Quinn put a couple more shots through the driver's door.

Jim stopped the RV on the shoulder about 200 yards ahead of where the squad car came to rest and checked the action in his mirrors and on his backup camera. Jack and Quinn went to check on the driver in the squad car. He was still alive, but badly wounded when they pulled him out of the car. The guy was definitely not a state trooper, he had white supremacist tattoos all over his arms and neck.

Jim hopped out of the RV and hurried back to where Jack and his team were checking the guy out. Quinn was searching the squad car for weapons while Jack tried to question the guy. The questioning was not productive, the guy just kept telling Jack to "Fuck off!" In the car, Quinn found an assault rifle, plenty of ammunition, a handgun, and a map of Minnesota with a bunch of places circled, some marked with a Z, and others marked with an X. Quinn studied the map for a few minutes and then brought it to Jack. "Take a look at this, there's a circle here, that's where that roadblock of cars was. The Blatnik and Bong bridges are marked with an X, so are the bridges by the border up north. And there's a Z right here, which is about where you first encountered this guy." He nodded towards the fake-trooper. "If these symbols mean what I think, we could use this map to get to the border without too many more surprises. If the map is accurate and these idiots don't go off script."

Jack nodded as he looked at the map. "The rest of our group should be waiting for us up ahead a ways. I don't want to leave them exposed too long. Let's get moving now. Looks clear on this road until Virginia. We can find a place to stop along the way and map out our route."

RJ pointed at the wounded fake-trooper. "Just leave him then?"

Jack nodded and started walking to his truck.

Jim stepped up to the militia member. "What reason could you possibly have for wanting to kill my kids?" He paused but got no response. "May God have mercy on your soul, but I wouldn't complain if you went the other way." Jim pulled out his gun and shot the man in the head, then walked away leaving him on the shoulder of the highway.

Jim started walking back to the RV. About halfway there his legs started to feel like jelly and he staggered a bit. After another ten feet or so he lurched into the grass and vomited – there wasn't much in there, but he felt a little better after getting it out. The Jeep pulled up next to him and he heard Quinn, "First time is the worst. Hope you don't have to get used to it." Quinn gave Jim a beat to gather himself then he said, "Your family needs you functional right now. Put what you did out of your mind. You can deal with it later. Time to move."

Jim looked at Quinn and nodded. Then he got moving.

29

∾

July 1 - Outside Calgary - evening

"Whoa, man. You killed someone. You weren't trained for that like those vets were. Are you okay? Have you come to grips with it?" Chad was genuinely concerned.

"Not to spoil the suspense, but that guy wasn't the only person I killed that day. I've justified it in my mind and I've asked for forgiveness almost every day. Now I don't think I need to ask for forgiveness because the people I killed would have killed my innocent kids without a second thought and justified it in their twisted, hateful version of pseudo-Christianity. They didn't need to be blocking our path that day. Hell, they didn't need to do any of the things that happened that day." He sighed. "I don't know if God just isn't paying attention anymore, like Chuck in *Supernatural*, if you've seen that show, but the help we got that day was of the temporal variety, not heavenly. Sometimes I wonder if God hasn't just abandoned America out of sheer embarrassment about the quality of the people who are most loudly claiming to be on his team." Jim shook his head. "Don't get me wrong, I prayed a bunch on June 6th and still pray pretty regularly, mostly that the good guys kill all the bad guys before there's nothing left of the U.S. Sometimes I ask for a little justice."

He took another short pause and stared off into the distance. "I used to just shake my head at the looney televangelists scamming old ladies out of their money, but the last ten years or so the grifting has gotten hateful and there seems to be no end to the people willing to give money to fake Christians that tell them what they want to hear. If God wants to finally strike down all the fake preachers who've funded their private jets convincing people that Jesus wants them to hate other people, I wouldn't be opposed to that either. The grifters clearly don't believe in the Bible or they'd realize that they're going to face judgment from their maker one day and St. Peter isn't going to just hand them the cup of eternal life after they've been the cause of so much misery to people Jesus loves down here. If you haven't gotten there in your reading yet, pay close attention to Matthew, Chapter 7, verses 21 to 23. I think about those verses a lot these days. I really hope Jesus actually said those words and meant them."

Chad smiled wryly, "Yeah, you might still have some issues you're dealing with."

Jim took a long drink of water. "I'm much better than I was three weeks ago. But it's going to be a long time before I can forgive the people who put us through all this. I may never get there. And I'm not ready to completely let my guard down. I have a family to look out for." He looked to be in deep thought. "But I am feeling much better."

After a brief pause, Chad asked, "So how many places do you think were marked on that map they pulled out of the squad car?"

Jim looked off into the distance, thinking. "Hmmm, there were the seven border crossings, the three bridges to Wisconsin, a bunch of bridges over the Mississippi River, a few roadblocks on highways, and maybe five or six places marked like there would be a fake cop watching the high-way. Maybe twenty to twenty-four markings that I saw. But I only saw the Northern half of the map. Don't know what was marked south of Duluth."

Chad nodded, "So, think about how many guys it would take to man all those places and blow all those bridges. You're probably talking about 70 to 100 militia members. Are they the same people who stayed up all night blowing up the power stations and shooting it out with the cops? If not, then you probably need to double the number. And that's just in Minnesota, north of Duluth. How many would they need around Minneapolis or some of the other cities in the southern part of the state? Then think about all the blue cities in the U.S. and the number of militia members it would take to surround those places and blow up their infrastructure. We can't be talking about only a few thousand people. It would have to be a lot more."

Jim was nodding, "All I really know about the militia stuff is what I saw in the media. The standoffs over cattle grazing, mines, and the wildlife refuge. Oh, and the Michigan stuff where the militia members went into the state capitol with their guns to intimidate lawmakers during COVID. Didn't they try to do that in Oregon too? I guess you know a lot more than I do about them. How many of them are there?"

Chad shook his head. "I don't know. A lot more than I would have thought a month ago. I still can't get my head around how much coordination this had to take. From what I already knew and what you're saying you experienced on the 6th, I'm leaning more into the idea that this had to be a conspiracy involving people at many levels of the government."

"Again, not to ruin the suspense, but I don't think anything that happened to my family the rest of that day is going to move the needle on your opinion about who caused this mess."

Chad nodded, "Let's get back to the 6th, if you don't mind."

30

June 6th - Highway 53 - early afternoon

Jack led the small convoy with Jim in the middle and the Jeep at the rear. After a few miles, Jack spotted the rest of their group in the parking lot of an abandoned restaurant. They all pulled in and Jack signaled for the drivers to come gather around.

Once he parked, Jim turned back and let Joy know they were going to be stopped for a few minutes and it would be a good time for the girls to take a bathroom break and stretch their legs. Then he got out and joined the rest of the group.

Jack had the newly acquired map spread out on the hood of the Jeep and was studying the markings. The approaches to all four of the border crossings in Western Minnesota were circled, which they determined meant they were blocked by an armed barricade of some sort. A number of the bridges over the Mississippi River were marked with an X, which they assumed meant the bridges were to be destroyed. There were Z markings on some of the main state highways, which indicated that they were guarded by an unknown number of militia members monitoring passing traffic. Jack started with their destination – the Piney border crossing was his first choice – and worked his way back along different routes while avoiding places with markings and trying to avoid travelling through any of the larger towns along the way.

Once he had the route figured out, he used a red pen to trace a winding combination of federal, state, county, and local roads from the Piney border crossing back to their current location. They had cell service, so Jim pulled up a satellite view of the area around the border crossing. There was a small airport with a runway that actually ran across the border and seemed to be part of the border complex. There was a farmhouse and barn across the highway from the airport. It was a wide open area with no trees or cover. Jim showed his phone to Jack. Then Jim pulled up the satellite view of the Tolstoi border crossing and showed that to Jack. The road leading to that crossing appeared to be surrounded by heavy forest crowding the highway without much space on either side of the road.

Jack nodded and turned to the group. "Okay, we're going to get off this highway and head west in a little while. Same formation as before. Make sure you don't lose track of the vehicle in front of you because we are going to be making a lot of turns along the way. I'll be in contact with RJ and Quinn," he held up some sort of walkie talkie, "but if anyone misses a turn it's going to slow us down and could put you in danger. Pay attention."

They all nodded that they understood and headed back to their vehicles. Carl walked with Jim. "Chuck just told me you took a couple of shots at that roadblock. He said he might have also put a stray shot through the back of your camper by accident." Jim looked surprised but didn't interrupt him. "Your camper seems to be attracting the wrong kind of attention. How is your family holding up?"

"They're scared. Those bullets that came through the side were really close to Joy. I didn't know Chuck took a shot at us too. I just want to get somewhere safe as soon as we can." Jim stopped walking and looked right at Carl. "Jack and his guys are the real deal. This would have been impossible without them. I can't thank you enough for bringing them in. If we get through this day, my family is going to owe them our lives."

"Let's get through this day first before you start writing IOUs." He lowered his voice. "That Paul seems a little squirrely to me. I don't think he wants to go to Canada, but LeAnn has Jennifer riding with her. If I were you, I'd try to keep an eye on LeAnn's car if you can because Paul might just cut and run somewhere, even without Jennifer." He looked up and saw that Jack was ready to go. "Whoops, gotta go. Good luck. Stay safe."

"You too." Jim went to the camper and hopped into the driver's seat. "Okay ladies we're moving again. Does everybody have water and snacks? If all goes well we may not stop again for quite a while."

"What does quite a while mean?" Joy was sitting on the couch with Alex. Alex had decided to be Deaf for the time being. Kelly was sitting on the bench seat of the dinette with her feet hanging down into the washtub. Joy had found Kelly's noise-cancelling headphones, and she was wearing them now. "And is it safe to sit up right now, at least for a little while? I don't want to take any risks, but sitting up for a while longer would be nice for all of us."

"Hopefully we won't need to stop for a couple hours. The route is going to take us off the main road, so there's going to be a lot of turning. You might want to have a puke noodle handy." They rarely went through a trip without someone, usually Joy, throwing up along the way, so there was a supply of air sickness bags in the organizer hanging off the back of the driver's seat.

"Well smart guy, there's a wall of steel between me and the puke bags." Jim had forgotten about the sheet of file cabinet pieces he had set up behind his seat to protect them. "Can you reach back and grab a few for us?"

He looked out the windshield and saw the Corvette was pulling out of the lot. He quickly turned and found the bags on the back of his seat and tossed them to Joy before turning back and heading for the exit. "Here we go. Just keep the girls below the windows while we're on the main highway. We turn left in like fifteen miles and after that you should all get back into your safe places. And be ready to move sooner if I say so."

Jim checked his mirrors and saw the Jeep was in its designated position. Knowing he had that safety blanket made him feel so much better.

He looked at the rearview mirror hanging from the windshield and saw that Joy and Alex were smooshed together signing something to each other. He couldn't see Kelly, which was good, that meant she was sitting down low like he had asked.

They got up to 65 mph and Jim could see the entire caravan on the long straight stretches of the highway. He let his mind wander a little bit thinking about all the times one of the ladies had to use a puke noodle over the years. There was the time Alex got so sick driving through the switchbacks on the way to Rocky Mountain National Park. The time Kelly got sick when the GPS took them zigzagging through rural Kansas, turning onto a different county road every couple miles. He thought about the day in Texas when Joy had such a terrible migraine. They got pulled over by the Border Patrol as they were leaving Big Bend National Park and Jim let the agent search the RV just to get moving quicker. Seeing Joy laying on the couch puking seemed to speed up the agent's search. Jim hadn't thought about Big Bend in a while. He wondered if it was a military camp now. When his family was there, the Rio Grande was just a trickling stream that he could have easily waded across. It was understandable why the Border Patrol needed a strong presence there and he didn't begrudge them for thinking an RV with all the shades drawn might be hiding some passengers who had crossed the river illegally. The border patrol agent had been intimidating, like he just knew they were doing something wrong.

He was almost as intimidating as the Capitol Police officer they encountered when they went to take pictures of the Capitol last summer. That guy's approach and tone made Jim feel like he had done something wrong just by being there. Jim wondered where that officer had been on January 6, 2021, because he seemed like he could have stopped the shenanigans that day by just standing in front of the door ordering people to leave. Jim thought that as intimidating as the Border Patrol officer and the Capitol Police officer were, he would take Jack over either of them any day if he needed someone to protect his family. They all exuded confidence, but Jim felt like the other guys took some pleasure in intimidating a dad vacationing with his wife and daughters. Jack was a real leader who so far had shown adaptability and decision-making skills in the face of real danger. He hadn't shown much in the way of emotion, but he hadn't been bullying to any of them either.

"How long until we turn?"

Jim snapped out of his woolgathering. He did this on long drives, got lost in thought and the next thing he knew, they were twenty miles down the road. This was not the day to get lost in thought though. He looked around to get his bearings. This was a highway he had driven many times. "Less than two miles, I think. Wait until after the turn to help the girls move."

They turned left onto a county road and headed west. It was a two-lane road with lots of tree cover on both sides and occasional driveways leading to homes or businesses. The road skirted them around Hibbing and then Jack started leading them on a circuitous route that included county roads, local roads, and occasional brief forays onto state or federal highways. Jim had a compass on his dashboard and monitored their direction frequently. For the most part they kept moving west and north, but occasionally they headed south.

There's a reason Minnesota is called the Land of 10,000 Lakes and it's not easy to plot a straight route from one point to another when there are hundreds of lakes in between. With the frequent turns and curvy roads, Jim only occasionally saw more than the red Corvette in front of him. He made sure to check his mirrors frequently to make sure the Jeep was still behind him and wasn't signaling that he was going the wrong way. The girls were tucked into their safe space and Joy was laying on the couch listening to a book. They had been driving for almost two hours on this stretch and everything was going fine. Jim had seen people in their yards mowing the grass and gardening. There had been kids playing in yards at houses they had passed. They were encountering other traffic going the other way. Out here, off the beaten path in the rural Northern Minnesota, life seemed to be pretty normal today. Jim wondered how long that would last. *How long can the rural parts of the country function if the cities are war zones? Will these people be forced to pick a side, or will they be able to stay here and live their lives? What would happen to us if we just pulled into one of the campgrounds up here and tried to check in for a month?* Jim assumed most people who had power and internet had to know what was going on in other parts of the state and the country.

He really would have liked to pull over and ask one of the people doing yardwork for their perspective. He wondered what these people were thinking when RJ and Quinn drove by in their Jeep, both in military garb, Quinn with a rifle ready. *Would the residents assume Quinn was a militia member or a soldier? Jim wondered if that was how Jack's team overtook the roadblock earlier today. Maybe they just drove up like they were in the militia and then started shooting and throwing grenades. Maybe they used drones. Maybe someday he'd find out.* He followed the Corvette through a left turn onto a dirt road. *Hope we're not on this too long, dirt roads and motorhomes do not go well together.*

After a minute or so on the dirt road, he checked the mirror and saw that the Jeep was flashing its headlights, so he stopped and rolled down his window. The Jeep pulled up next to him and Quinn said, "We weren't supposed to turn back there. Turn around and wait for us back at the intersection. We'll go after Paul."

"Carl said he thought Paul might bail on us," Jim replied. "Wish he hadn't picked this narrow dirt road."

"Turn around carefully. We'll be back soon." The Jeep took off up the dirt road.

Jim checked his surroundings. "Honey, we have to do a Y turn here that might turn into a ZZZ turn. There's going to be a lot of back and forth because this is a narrow road, and I don't want to end up in a ditch." Joy gave him a thumbs-up.

Jim started working the RV through turning around. There were ditches on both sides close to the road so that limited the amount he could turn on each rotation. He was about three-fourths of the way done when a couple of dirt bikes came roaring towards them from the direction of the road they had turned off. Jim still had his window down, so he heard them coming before he saw them. He looked toward the sound and noticed there were two riders on the first bike, both wearing helmets with full face protection. When he saw them, he knew the situation was going downhill fast.

The passenger on the first bike was aiming a handgun at the RV. Jim pulled out his gun and took careful aim. At least the bikes were moving on a bumpy road and the gunman was unlikely to be able to hold his aim well. Jim was sitting and could take a more accurate shot. "Everybody plug your ears, there's going to be shooting." Joy dropped to the floor near the girls and made sure they were lying flat in the washtub. The biker fired a shot that hit a couple feet behind Jim and went right through the wall and through the camper behind Jim but in front of his family. It was well in front of where the girls were and too high to hit anyone, but it also missed all of the protection Jim had mounted earlier so it could have done serious damage. Jim aimed for the chest of the driver of that bike and said a silent prayer as he pulled the trigger. He got the driver in the shoulder and the bike turned wildly, throwing both riders off and onto the road.

The second bike was getting close now, but Jim was worried about the passenger with the gun, so he carefully fired two shots that both appeared to hit the gunman before he could get up. Jim could hear screaming coming from behind him, and knew the loud gunshots had shocked Kelly's sensitivities, but he had to focus completely on the immediate threat before he could think about helping his family. He turned his attention to the second bike. The rider was somehow holding a handgun while also keeping the bike upright on the bumpy dirt road. The rider fired a couple of quick shots that went high and punched through the sleeping area above the driver's cab, missing Jim by at least five feet, but then the guy had to steady his bike. Jim put a shot right into the rider's chest from less than thirty feet away. The bike went down and the man and the bike skidded another ten or fifteen feet down the dirt road before coming to a stop. Jim quickly hopped out of the RV and ran over to the closest biker. Not wanting to take a chance that the helmet the gunman was wearing might stop a bullet, Jim hunkered down and shot the guy right in the heart. He looked up to see if either of the other two bikers were moving. The driver of the first bike was trying to roll over. Jim figured he was at least a hundred feet away. Taking careful aim, Jim squeezed off two shots at the guy, hitting him once for sure. *How many bullets did he have left?* He holstered his gun and grabbed the gun dropped by the second biker. Trying to cover the open ground as quickly as possible, he ran the hundred feet to where the first two bikers were down. They were both still alive, but neither of them was moving. First, he kicked their guns out of reach, then he shot each of them once through the heart.

Jim stood in the road, his heart and mind racing. *These guys just showed up shooting without even checking to see who he was or where he was from. How did they know he wasn't here to check on a relative who lives down this road? Did they just assume he was someone they needed to eliminate? How would they know I'm not on their side? And what side were they on?* Looking around he noticed the dirt bike closest to him had a militia sticker on the fender next to a sticker with a cross and the words, "Jesus Saves." *Okay, they're on the other side and the guy who owns the bike flunked out of Sunday School. But how did they know I'm not on their side? Was it possible the fake trooper or someone who survived at the roadblock was able to let the whole militia network know about the caravan with the RV? If that's the case, there might be more surprise ambushes ahead for them.*

He looked at the three guns from the bikers. The one he was holding had been fired what, five times, maybe six. He threw it into the ditch. The gun from the passenger of the first bike had only been fired once, but he wasn't sure he knew how to work it. The gun from the driver of the first bike was similar to his own gun. He popped out the clip and it was full. He decided to keep that gun and he tossed the other gun into the ditch. Hurrying back to the RV, he scanned in all directions and didn't see anyone or any other movement. He got back in the RV, letting Joy know it was him and that the bad guys were dead. Now he heard the girls crying and Joy trying to comfort them and tell them they were safe. A feeling of helplessness took over as it hit him how bad this situation could have been if there had been more bad guys, or they had better weapons. He quickly said a silent prayer of thanks and finished getting his rig turned around. Nothing came to mind that he could say to his family that would be comforting at the moment. By the time he had the RV pointed down the road, he could see the Jeep coming up behind him in the rearview mirror.

He stared at the mirror for a few seconds looking for the Corvette, but the Jeep was all alone.

As soon as RJ pulled up next to the RV, he and Quinn saw the wrecked bikes and bodies in the road. "What the hell happened?" Quinn was not expecting this. Apparently, they hadn't heard the shooting, which struck Jim as odd. *How far did they go before they turned around? And what happened to Paul?*

"Those guys rode up shooting and I shot back." Jim pointed above and behind him to the holes in the side of the camper. "Luckily they only had pistols."

"You're the luckiest guy I've ever seen whose been shot at by five different guys in two hours. Stay behind us until we catch up with the group. We'll clear the road up ahead."

Jim gave him a thumbs-up. RJ pulled forward and moved the second bike off the road while Quinn pulled the body out of the road. They pulled forward again and did the same thing with the other bike and bodies. Jim took the time to switch out his almost empty clip with the full one and put his newly acquired gun in the storage cubby where he could reach it. He was really thankful for the time he had spent at the range learning how to shoot way back when he acquired his guns. All these years it had seemed like a waste of time and money, but that investment was paying off for his family today.

RJ took a left onto the blacktop at the main road and Jim followed at a distance that would allow RJ and Quinn to hear if he honked for help. He was again in that uncomfortable position of being at the rear without any cover. He yelled back to the family. "Hey, we're back on the main road and the bad guys are gone. Probably a couple hours to the border. RJ and Quinn are going to be right here for us. It's going to be okay." He felt terrible lying to his kids like that, but wanted them to think he was confident in their safety.

"We just got scared when you had to shoot your gun, dad. We were worried about you, dad. Now that you're safe, we're feeling better." Joy was speaking in a very calm, even tone, signing to Alex as she talked. She had to be just as scared as the girls and Jim, but she wasn't showing any fear or negative emotion at all. Jim thought her performance was amazing, and it did seem to be helping the girls to settle down. "We're fine back here dad. You focus on your driving. We can handle this, can't we girls?"

"I love you all. I'm going to focus on the road now." Maintaining his following distance, their two-vehicle caravan worked its way through more turns than Jim could believe. *How did these guys know which turns to make? Was Chuck telling them over the radio? Was it safe to be using a radio to announce our route out here? Maybe they had a map with the route marked just like Jack.* Jim couldn't remember seeing them with a map, but plenty of stuff happened today that he wasn't a part of. RJ drove like he knew the way and that was good enough for Jim. They drove and drove without incident. The only towns they went through were of the one or no-stop sign variety, anything larger they avoided by using side roads. Jim completely lost track of where they were and the towns they saw were so small, he had never heard of any of them anyway. His sense of direction was always suspect (that's why he had a compass on the dashboard), so RJ could have been leading him anywhere and he would have followed blindly. Jim tensed up a little every time he saw another vehicle, but they didn't have any trouble. After a couple hours, the Jeep pulled off the left side of the road into a gravel lot, drove around a long-abandoned building that might have at one time been a farm supply store, and pulled into the gravel parking area behind the building. There was the rest of the group, standing around chatting while Jack was inspecting a weapon that Jim thought looked capable of shooting through a brick wall.

Jim parked the RV in a position to make a quick escape if they needed to. Behind the parking lot was an open field for at least 500 yards, so they would see anyone approaching from that direction. The building shielded them from view by anyone driving on the road, but that meant they could be ambushed by someone coming around the building catching them by surprise. After he parked, Jim noticed that Chuck was acting as lookout from behind a pile of abandoned pallets across the driveway they had just used to come around the building. From that vantage point,

Chuck could see the entire area in front of the building so nobody could sneak around either side. That made Jim feel better.

"Hey, we're in a place that might be safe for a while if anyone needs to use the bathroom or get something to eat or drink." Jim looked back to see how his family was doing.

"How much farther to the border?" Joy had stood up in the back to stretch her legs. She was unbuckling the seatbelts across the top of the washtub to free the girls.

"Don't know. I think we're pretty close. Do you want to come out with me while I find out?"

She shook her head, "I'm going to help the girls get something to eat and make sure they use the bathroom. We're going to stretch a bit in here after being so cramped for so long. You're sure it's safe?"

He shrugged. "We're in a place that nobody can sneak up on us unless we let them. I think it's Okay to get up for a while." He looked out the window. "Jack is looking this way. I should get out there and find out what's going on." Jim hopped out the driver's door and hurried over to where Jack was standing with the group.

Once Jack had the entire group around him, he laid out his plans. "The border is about ten minutes away. Things have been quiet for the last seventy miles, but we suspect that's going to change on the last stretch before the border. RJ, Quinn, and I are going to take a trip to scout what's up ahead and see if we can clear you a path to the border. We're going to take two vehicles this time. Chuck is going to keep a radio and he knows where to go from here. When we give him the all clear, he'll lead the way followed by Carl then Jim. To save time, Chuck will brief you on what to do after we leave. If we're successful, we'll take out everything in your path and you'll have clear sailing to Canada, but I can't promise you that. You may need to drive through some stuff to get through the border. Either way, this is probably the last time we'll see each other until you come back home, so good luck."

They all shook hands and wished each other luck. Jim's eyes welled up as he thanked Jack, RJ, and Quinn one by one. He asked them to thank Steve when they got back to Duluth.

This time the Jeep went first with Jack following in his truck. Jim said a silent prayer for their safety, then he and Carl joined Chuck at the lookout.

"Sorry about Paul," Jim started, not knowing what else to say.

Chuck had a sarcastic smile. "Good riddance to that guy. I've been trying for years to get Jenny to drop that loser. Who knew all it took was a militia overthrowing society."

Not knowing how to follow that up, Carl tried. "So, Jack said you'd tell us what's going to happen next."

Chuck nodded. "Yep. So, depending on what they find at the border they're going to give me a color-coded direction. Green means we just roll up Highway 89 and zip up to the border station like an ordinary day. That's best-case scenario, and seems unlikely. Yellow means we approach on the dirt roads to the east and jump onto 89 right before the border station. We might have to do some off-roading depending on what things look like when we get there. Orange gets interesting. That plan has us coming up a dirt road from the west, turning onto a dirt or grass driveway – it's hard to tell from the satellite photos on google maps - then driving across a field onto the runway of the little airport and either crossing into Canada on the runway or on the taxiway, depending on what we encounter. Red means they can't get us through here, but they're coming back, and we have to try a different crossing. Purple is bad. That means we can't get through and we're on our own because they aren't going to be able to get away clean. I don't think that will happen. Jack is," he took a long pause, "I don't know how to explain it, but he's like superhuman. I wouldn't want to be on the other side of him when he has his arsenal out and free reign to use it. I like our chances with those guys on our side."

They just stood there for a few moments, all of them thinking about the situation. Then Carl spoke up. "Hey Chuck, you've been on lookout for a while. I'll take next watch, but can I come back in five? I really need to relieve myself."

"Take your time. I'm good here for a little bit longer." He looked at Jim. "You just got here, so you should spend some time with your family.

If our stay here drags out, you might need to take a turn, but me and Carl can handle the watch for a while."

Jim nodded. He and Carl started walking back towards the vehicles. Carl spoke first. "Word is that you took a few more bullets to the camper on that wrong turn. Is everybody okay?"

"Yeah, nothing hit within a few feet of any of us, but it was scary. I'd be good if I never had to shoot or be shot at again for the rest of my life."

Carl had a grim look. "Good luck with that. Maybe after today. Not sure you're going to get through the next stretch without pulling your weapon." They were coming up to Carl's SUV and Carl pointed at the rear passenger door. "Just so you don't feel too special, I took a couple in the side here, too."

Jim squatted down and looked closer at the bullet holes. "Looks like small caliber stuff. Was it a kid with a BB gun?"

"Look at you, joking in the face of danger. We sound just like characters in a war movie, except we have wives and kids to protect. These were from those same bikers that chased you down. They were sitting on the side of the road and put a couple shots into my truck and at least one into LeAnn's car – her rear passenger door window got hit. That might be what caused Paul to turn off. If he saw them shooting at us, he may have done a quick turn before he got to where they were."

That scenario got Jim thinking. *Maybe all was for the best with the wrong turn. It scared his kids, but who knows how different the situation might have been with three gunmen sitting on the side of the road taking target practice at his huge RV as he drove by. They might have killed him right there. Nothing he could do about it now, so no sense dwelling on it.* "Man, we are lucky we're all still alive with what we've been through today. Let's hope it keeps up."

"Amen to that. Go see how your kids are doing. I'll talk to you later."

Jim walked back to the camper.

31

July 1 - Outside Calgary - evening

"Okay, I need to take a break for a couple minutes. Is there privacy behind your camper?" Jim was practically dancing in his seat.

Chad chuckled, "As much privacy as you're going to need. There's a big tree back there that I've been marking since I got here."

Jim got up and walked around behind the camper. Chad broke the silence. "I hadn't spent much time thinking about how even some parts of blue states might not have been affected at all by what was going on in the cities. But hearing your story, now I wonder if there are rural areas where daily life, even now, is pretty much the same as it was before. There might be big parts of red states like Montana where you wouldn't even know people were getting killed in other parts of the country. I don't know how well I could have blended in there, but maybe I didn't need to leave the U.S. to avoid all the violence and death. Too late to do anything about it now, and at least here I don't have to be constantly looking over my shoulder worried about an armed militia member showing up at my campsite."

Jim came back. "Yeah. I feel pretty safe up here, even without my guns.

Maybe, especially because I don't need my guns anymore. If I go back to the U.S., I'm going to feel the need to buy guns again."

"I guess what happened to your guns is going to be a part of the rest of the story, right?"

Jim nodded. "Oh yeah. I won't leave that part out. Just let me get a drink of water and I think I can get the rest of the way through the 6th."

"Take your time. I'm not going anywhere."

Jim started back up. "So, I went back to the camper and hugged my wife and kids for a good five minutes. The girls were a mess. I may have had to shoot people and defend our camper with bullets, but they hadn't just had a fun RV ride listening to music and playing games on their iPads. Their systems weren't made for the kind of stressors that the trip was putting on them. Kelly especially was just a mess emotionally. Joy and I had to explain to them that they were going to have to spend another hour or so riding in the washtub, and then we could get rid of it forever. After a little family bonding time, they seemed to be resigned to going along, although we did promise them future benefits like extra screen time, lunches at I-Hop, and a campground with a pool. We were ready to promise anything, but preferred not to outright lie to them."

32

June 6th - Northern Minnesota - evening

Once the delicate negotiations over future benefits for their cooperation were completed, Kelly wanted to be alone for a while. She wanted to go to her sleeping area over the cab, but Jim suggested the bedroom in the back as a better place for her to decompress right now. Alex was Deaf right then and she sat at the far end of the couch, with her eyes closed. That was a new behavior for Alex, but after the day they'd had, it was an easy way for her to shut out the rest of the world. Jim dug around in the cupboards and found some granola bars since he couldn't remember the last time he ate. Sitting down on the couch, he suddenly felt exhausted from the lack of sleep and the long, stressful night and day. "Hey honey, can I have one of your cold coffees? I could use a little pick-me-up right now."

Joy grabbed a coffee out of the fridge and unscrewed the cap, handing it to Jim. "You can have all of them if they keep you awake long enough to get us somewhere on the other side of the border. They have Walmart in Manitoba. We can buy as many as I want tomorrow."

"Thanks babe. I'm just going to eat these bars and drink this, then I'm going to keep moving so I don't drop off. I want to cover the new holes in the sides before the mosquitoes come out tonight and we have real trouble. Don't want to have to use the mosquito net to sleep tonight if we can avoid it."

Joy sat down between Jim and Alex and cuddled up to Jim, "How much farther to Canada?"

"Jack said the border is ten minutes away. He took his team to clear the path for us and is going to radio back to Chuck when it's time for us to go."

Joy snuggled in closer and whispered, "Are we going to make it?"

Jim whispered back, "Chuck thinks Jack's guys are superheroes. I think they'll make a mess of whatever's in the way, but we might have to run a gauntlet to get to the border, then hope like hell the Canadians don't shoot us from their side. I don't think we're going to just get to drive up to the border station like tourists. But, yes, I think we're going to make it. I think by tomorrow night we'll be at a campground with a swimming pool cooking s'mores by a campfire. And next week we'll be in the Canadian Rockies camping by a mountain lake like we did that time in Banff."

Jim leaned over and tossed his empty bottle into the garbage can. He turned back and they embraced. The movement got the attention of Alex, who opened her eyes and looked at them briefly. Jim smiled at her, but she just turned away and closed her eyes before going back into her own thoughts. *Just get through this day, then we can all get back to who we were before.*

Jim stood up and went to the drawer under the stove. He dug around for a minute and pulled out a roll of white duct tape. "I'm going to get the exterior holes first, then I'll see how the damage looks in here." He went out the door and started taping over the bullet holes in the sides of the RV.

Jim was on his step ladder covering the holes in the over the cab sleeping area above the driver's door when Chuck came trotting over. "Quinn gave the signal, it's orange."

Jim was surprised. "Wow, that seems quick. I thought it would take longer."

"Nope, we've got to move now before the other guys can find reinforcements. I'll lead the way, you follow Carl. Stay as close to Carl as you can, and we may need to go fast, so have your kids buckle up."

"We'll be ready in two minutes. Have you told Carl?"

"Heading over there now. Good luck. See you in Canada, eh?"

That got a chuckle out of Jim. "I think your Canadian needs some work. Stay safe Chuck."

They shook hands and Chuck headed across the parking lot.

Jim went around the camper and opened the door. "We're leaving in two minutes, honey. Can you get the girls into their safe spot and buckle them up? I need to pack some things away out here."

Joy came out of the bathroom. "Already? It feels like we just got here."

"Chuck got the call. He knows where to go. There's going to be some cross-country driving, so make sure they have pillows and blankets under them, it could get bumpy."

She sighed. "Okay. Sixty minutes and we're safe. You promised. Don't be a liar, Jim."

Jim didn't know how to respond, so he shut the door and quickly stored his step ladder and supplies in the storage compartment. Looking across the parking lot, he saw Carl and Julie hugging Chuck and LeAnn before they got into their vehicles. Jennifer was in the back seat of Chuck's car already. Chuck and Carl got into their respective driver's seats and Jim wondered if their wives were proficient with their weapons. Chuck pulled out and around the building with Carl following closely.

"Here we go ladies. One more stretch of driving then we'll be in Canada." Jim opened the little cubby between the seats and pulled out the gun he took from the biker, made sure it was ready to shoot, and shoved it into the storage compartment in the driver's door where he could reach it if he needed to while driving. Then he got the RV moving, staying close to Carl once they got on the paved road.

Jim looked at the sky. The events of the day had warped his sense of how much time had elapsed since they left Duluth. It was definitely evening. The sky had a pinkish hue that told Jim sunset was near but they probably had a good hour plus of daylight left. He wondered if their final escape might be easier if it was a little darker. Code orange meant they were going to come in from the west and cross a grassy field onto the runway which was to the west of the highway and the border station. Maybe they would have an advantage with the sun behind them blinding the bad guys as they drove up. No sense in speculating about it though, he would know soon enough.

Chuck drove at a faster speed on the back roads than Jim cared for in the RV. Jim focused on keeping the RV on the road and as close to Carl as he could, but he fell back a few times when the road got too rough to keep the RV up to speed. Chuck noticed Jim's troubles and slowed down to let the RV catch up. When Jim let his eyes come up from the road immediately in front of him, he saw that there was smoke rising maybe a mile away. That had to be where Jack and his guys were doing battle. Jim rolled down both of the front windows and now he could hear guns firing, including some louder booms that Jim thought were probably made by the weapon Jack had been inspecting earlier. He hoped Jack was shooting that thing through whatever defenses the bad guys were hiding behind. Every dead bad guy was one less that would be around to shoot at his family.

Once Jim caught up to Carl, Chuck sped up a bit and the road curved to the east. As they came around the curve, the fighting was in front of them, still at least half a mile away. The ground between them and the fight was mostly open farmland with a few small stands of trees. He couldn't see much from here because the land rose a bit in between them and the fighting, but there wasn't going to be much cover when they got closer. Suddenly, Jim thought all the open land was a terrible circumstance. *How were they going to sneak around this gunfight when the land was wide open?*

Chuck took a left onto a dirt farm road and they still couldn't see the fighting yet, but it was close. Their vehicles were kicking up dust and dirt that would have to be visible if anyone looked in their direction. They were going to be sitting ducks once they got past the next little stand of trees. Jim quickly turned back to his family, "This is going to be the worst part. I love you all so much. Stay down."

Chuck had sped up once he passed the trees because there was no turning back for them now. Carl kept pace with Chuck, but Jim couldn't get the RV to speed up on the crappy farm road. Carl was pulling away from them and there wasn't anything Jim could do. After what seemed like an interminable wait, he finally hit a smooth patch of road and the RV picked up a little speed. Jim looked over at the battle, which was really close now. He could see everything from this distance. There were burning pickup trucks and a bulldozer blocking the highway. The vehicles in the roadblock covered the highway and the area around the road for a good twenty feet on either side of the blacktop. Most of the vehicles in the roadblock appeared to be severely damaged.

The highway bisected the road they were about to turn onto at a 45 degree angle about 300 yards ahead of them. Jim could see a couple guys ducked down behind the bulldozer blade shooting both to the east and to the southeast. Jack's guys must have split up and attacked from two sides. There were trees and farmhouses in both directions that the bad guys were shooting towards. Jack and his guys must be in those trees. As Jim turned right onto the final approach to the battle, the bulldozer blade was struck by automatic weapons fire forcing the men to duck down behind it. "Covering fire," Jim muttered. He looked back at the road in front of him and saw Chuck turning left onto the grass up ahead. Back to the battle, a drone came crashing down on the bulldozer followed by a small explosion.

Carl turned left onto the grass and was racing towards the runway, about thirty yards behind Chuck. Jim finally turned off the road still more than a hundred yards behind Carl. He started to think that this plan might just work when Chuck's car was hit by a fusillade of bullets through the windshield in a matter of seconds just as he was about to pull onto the runway.

Chuck lost control and the car roared right across the runway at a high speed and crashed into the trees on the other side. The shots had come from the trees directly in front of them, but they had no choice but to keep going now. Maybe they got lucky and Chuck's car ran over the shooter. Carl's SUV hit the paved runway and angled left to follow the pavement. Julie leaned out the passenger window of the SUV and started firing an AR-15 at the tree line. Jim hoped she was aiming at something and was a good shot. He couldn't see anything but Chuck's wrecked car.

Now that Carl was on the runway, he had the SUV going as fast as he could. Julie was still shooting, and Jim appreciated every shot she took. Jim was almost to the runway, but Carl was really getting away from him now. He was going to lose Julie's covering fire way before he got through the danger zone. Carl passed the taxiway and stayed on the runway. Jim now saw there were Canadian troops and military vehicles on the other side of the border at the far end of the runway. The soldiers had weapons out, ready to defend their border.

As Carl was about to cross the border, Julie tossed her gun out the window and put her arms out. Carl's vehicle drove past the first line of Canadian troops and vehicles and Jim lost sight of it.

As soon as the RV got onto the paved runway, Jim pulled his gun from the holster and started firing at the trees out the passenger window trying not to hit Chuck's car in case anyone in there somehow survived to this point. He couldn't see anyone in the trees, but the covering fire had worked for Julie, so he hoped it would work for him too. He had the gas pedal floored and was about a quarter of the way up the runway, slowly picking up speed. He had fired four shots at the tree line when there was a thump at the back of the RV followed by a small explosion that rocked the camper like an earthquake pulling his foot off the gas pedal. Joy and the girls all started screaming after that jolt.

Jim looked down at the screen showing the backup camera and there were pieces of what must have been a small drone spraying through the air. It must have hit the back wall and bounced off before the explosives went off. He got his foot back on the gas pedal and willed the RV to go faster. He didn't make it another fifty feet before the driver's side of the bedroom wall was drilled with small arms fire coming from the trees behind them and to the west. Letting go of the wheel and steering with his left knee, Jim grabbed the second gun out of the door with his left hand, reached out the window, and started shooting towards the tree line on that side of the runway while continuing to take intermittent shots through the passenger window at the stand of trees to his east with the gun in his right hand. He wasn't going to hit anything, and had to be careful not to shoot his own camper behind him, but he wanted to make the bad guys take cover. It seemed to Jim like the RV was driving in molasses. Then there was a clang behind him. He knew immediately the washtub had been hit.

"ARE THE GIRLS OKAY??" He yelled, while making sure to keep the gas pedal floored. The damn runway seemed so long. There was still plenty of screaming back behind him. The RV continued to pick up speed as they got past the taxiway, following the route Carl took. "JOY!! ARE THE GIRLS OKAY?"

He finally heard movement back there, but she still hadn't answered. He kept shooting intermittently out each side to provide covering fire without being able to look at where he was shooting. Finally, Joy answered. "They're okay. The tub is dented, but not punctured."

They were almost to the border when the automatic weapon from the trees to the east opened up again. At least twenty bullets drilled the rear and passenger side of the bedroom, destroying the windows on the side and rear and blowing out the outside rear tire on the passenger side. Jim's tire warning system began to beep loudly, and the RV lurched to the right. Jim threw his guns onto the passenger seat and grabbed the wheel with both hands to regain control just as they finally crossed the border. The shooter in the trees was now shooting into Canada, and the Canadian military returned fire and launched mortars at the trees. The shooting from the trees stopped.

The Canadians let Jim drive past their front line and all the way to the end of the runway, then they surrounded the RV. Jim stuck his arms out the window, "Don't shoot. There are children in here with me. We just want to be safe."

A soldier opened the door and let Jim step out on his own. "Where's your firearm?"

"They're on the passenger seat, two of them. There's one more in the little storage compartment between the seats. Can somebody check on my wife and kids? We took a lot of lead at the end there." He turned his head and yelled back into the camper. "Joy! Are you guys okay!"

After a brief pause. "We're okay. Is it safe to come out?"

Jim was holding his arms over his head. He looked at the soldier who seemed to be in charge. The soldier nodded. "Ma'am you can come out. If you have any weapons leave them in the RV."

Joy and the girls came out the side door and came around the RV. Joy spoke quickly as they exited the camper. "I'm with a Deaf child and an autistic child. They might not obey orders. Don't hurt them." Kelly was wearing her noise-cancelling headphones and looked like she didn't know what planet she was on. Alex ran up and hugged Jim. She seemed to think he was about to be arrested.

The soldier took charge. "Do you have passports?"

Jim nodded. "They're in a zippered bag in the sunshade on the passenger side. Are you going to let us stay for a while? I'm not real keen on going back to the U.S. right now."

The soldier pointed to an SUV. "Hop in. We'll give you a ride to the border station. I'll have someone bring your documents after we search the vehicle. Are the keys still in the ignition?"

Jim handed over the keys. "Let me know if you need help with any of the storage compartments. It's the funny looking key with the blue on it."

They all squeezed into the back seat of the vehicle for the short drive to the border station. Joy looked over at Jim. "Did everybody else already go in?"

Jim shook his head. "Carl and Julie crossed a little bit before us. I guess they're in the building already, but I didn't see their vehicle when we stopped. Chuck and LeAnn didn't make it across."

She frowned but understood this wasn't a discussion to have in front of the girls. They rode the rest of the way in shell-shocked silence.

The soldier led them into the border station where they found Julie sitting in a plastic chair in the lobby, sobbing. Joy rushed over to her. "What's wrong? Where's Carl?"

Between sobs Julie let them know that Carl had taken a bullet through the driver's door. It got him in the left side and the soldiers had rushed him to a medical facility. She didn't know how bad it was, and she couldn't leave to be with him until she got processed here. Joy hugged Julie and tried to comfort her.

Jim helped the girls to a couple of chairs and crouched down in front of them. He couldn't think of anything to say to them at this moment and they looked like they didn't know what was going on around them. Alex was Deaf and Jim hoped Joy had the cochlear implant hardware in her pocket. Kelly was completely checked out.

Here they were, nine neighbors who left for Canada (ten if you counted Paul), and only five of them made it to the border station while the rest of the people they travelled with were either dead or in surgery and potentially dying, and who knows what happened to Paul. If he knew this morning there was only a fifty percent chance of any of them making it, would he have made the trip? He was probably going to have some serious survivor's guilt in the future, but he hoped the girls wouldn't. They had nothing to do with any of the decisions made today or the actions taken. The precautions he and Joy had taken to protect the kids on the drive had worked, but mostly it was just luck that they were all in one piece when the others in their group didn't make it through this day. Now he needed to make sure they could stay in Canada.

A border officer came out and took Julie into the back. Joy came over and squatted down in front of the girls. She hugged them while they waited. After about five minutes, a soldier came through the door and handed Jim the bag with their documents. A couple minutes later they were taken into an office to meet with a border officer. The officer looked at their documents and asked them their reason for visiting Canada. Jim's jaw dropped open at that one. Joy gave him a look that said, "Keep your smart-ass commentary to yourself for once."

Jim explained that their hometown was overrun by a militia that was killing citizens and that Canada was a safe place to take a vacation until law enforcement back in the states got things under control. Jim told him to look at the ferry schedules in the bag which showed that their vacation was planned well in advance of today's events, and that seemed to be good enough for the guy. They went through the normal questions about how long they planned to stay (maybe thirty days), did they have any drugs or firearms in their vehicle (none), how much alcohol they were transporting (none), and something about dairy products (there was some shredded cheese in the refrigerator of their camper). Their answers seemed to satisfy the guy. He told them to enjoy their stay and let them go.

As they walked out of the building, Jim couldn't contain himself. "That was freaking insane. That guy treated our entry today like any old border crossing on a Tuesday in June. He rushed through our interview like he had a big backlog to deal with. Is this Canada or have we entered the *Twilight Zone*?"

A solder walked up to them as they came out the door. He handed Jim his keys. "Your RV is over there." He pointed. "You're going to have to drive slow until you get a new tire. There's a lot of damage to the back end and the rear bedroom. You should find a repair shop soon. Welcome to Canada."

Jim was speechless for once and Joy took the opportunity to speak first. "Did the woman who was with us leave yet? Do you know where they took her husband?"

"Yes ma'am. She drove away a few minutes ago. Her husband was taken to Winnipeg, but I don't know which hospital."

Jim turned to the soldier. "Thank you for letting us into your country in our time of need. I hope you can keep those lunatics at bay on the other side of your border." Turning back to his family. "Okay ladies, let's see if we can find a place to stay for the night."

Approaching the RV from the rear, Jim assessed the damage that he hadn't seen in the rush after they crossed the border. The rear wall was bowed in and had a dark stain from the explosion, a taillight was shattered, there was the one tire blown out and there were at least a dozen bullet holes near the back corner of the RV on the passenger side with both the side and rear bedroom windows shattered. On the driver's side, the rear area had fewer holes, but it had taken some hits. Moving forward on the driver's side, he found the hole made by the bullet that almost got his family. From where it entered, it must have gone through the cupboard under the sink. They were lucky that shot had to travel through a wall, a cupboard full of food, the cupboard wall, and the storage area under the dinette seat before it hit where the girls were hiding. Probably wrecked some of our food, but that's an issue for later. He wondered if the water tank was still intact and how well the stuff in their rear storage compartment had survived. Nothing he could do about any of that here and now. The border station was miles from an RV repair shop or a place to stay. All he could do was try to limp his rig to civilization.

They all got in and took their usual seats. Joy sat in the passenger seat for this trip so the girls could lay down on their seats. Alex curled up in the fetal position on the couch and Kelly splayed out on the bench seat of the dinette. Joy made sure the girls were buckled up and Jim started the RV moving. With the tire gone, the rig pulled to the right like crazy and the rear end made some uncomfortable noises while they drove. Jim disabled the tire warning system so it would stop beeping every thirty seconds and slowly worked his way through the Manitoba farmland towards Winnipeg. While they were driving, Joy tried calling both of their moms to see how they were doing and let them know what had happened to their granddaughters. Neither of them answered, but Joy was able to leave voicemail messages explaining that they were safe in Canada and would keep trying to reach out.

It was after midnight when they pulled into a Walmart just outside of Winnipeg. Joy helped Kelly get up into her sleeping area, hoping she wouldn't discover any bullet fragments in her bedding, but it was too late to do much about it at this point. If they had to deal with a *Princess and the Pea* situation during the night, they would handle that when it came up. Jim went into the bedroom and used half a roll of duct tape to cover the broken windows from the inside. He lifted up the end of the bed and looked at the water tank. From what he could see, there was still water in there and there wasn't any standing water on the outside of the tank. Maybe they had lucked out and the tank was intact. He went outside and used the duct tape to cover the bullet holes in the bedroom walls. Out of habit, he opened up the rear storage compartment and pulled out the vinyl windshield cover. It seemed to be intact, so he set it up on the windshield for the night. Jim remembered to grab the hand-held vacuum out of the storage compartment before going in for the night. By the time he got back inside, Alex was asleep on the couch in her sleeping bag and Kelly was tucked into her sleeping area.

Joy was in the bedroom looking at the mess. The top mattress had taken a few hits and there was some stuffing poking out of the holes. There was broken glass on top of the mattress that Jim vacuumed up. Joy swept the debris on the floor around the bed so they wouldn't cut their feet on anything, but it was a quick job by a blind person, so Jim would need to do a follow-up in the morning. Some of the cabinetry was in rough shape with bullet holes and shards of wood sticking out. Joy held up Jim's backpack, showing him that a bullet had gone in, but didn't appear to have come out the other side. Probably not good news for the laptop computer inside. "It's late and I don't have much energy left. Can we just make the bed and try to get some sleep? We can deal with the rest of this mess when we get up."

Jim nodded. "We need to do some things tomorrow that are pretty urgent. I'm going to set my alarm for 8:00. I want to be at a bank by 9 and then we have to find a place to get some RV repairs done. We may have to stay in a motel for a while."

"Just help me make the bed. You can even sleep in your clothes for all I care right now. I didn't have a chance to check your suitcase to see if you have any clothes without bullet holes. Did you lock all the doors?"

"We're all locked up. Time to sleep."

Jim pulled the bedding from the overhead cabinet, and they made the bed in silence. Jim set his alarm for the next morning and set his phone on the counter on his side of the bed. As he got comfortable in the bed, he turned to Joy, "Good night you. We're safe now."

"I really hope that's true. Good night."

33

July 1 - Outside Calgary -
after sunset

"So, you know a bit about what happened after the 6th already. The next morning, I did some banking and found a place to get some RV repairs done so my rig runs right and doesn't look like it went through a war. We were able to find Carl and Julie at a hospital in Winnipeg, and Carl's prognosis was good at that time, but Julie was very cold to us. We assumed she was mad because it was our idea to go to Canada and that's how Carl ended up getting shot, but I don't know that for sure and we haven't seen them since. We all were dealing with our own demons at the time. She was close to LeAnn, and she had to feel terrible about what happened to Norm and his son. So much pain and suffering to people who lived on our street. And that was just the first day. Who knows how much death and suffering has happened since." He sighed and shook his head. "Anyway, we scrapped our plans to visit Newfoundland and Labrador to conserve our cash and have mostly bummed around Western Canada and the Canadian Rockies for the last few weeks instead."

Chad looked thoughtful. "Now I understand what you said this morning about incredible luck. Your family was lucky or has a guardian angel looking over it or something. Whatever it is, a lot of stuff had to come together just right for you to make that trip in one piece. I was caught off guard this morning when you said you made the trip on the 6th, mostly because of what I had heard and how I pictured things in my head. I thought your trip to the border must have been tough, especially in a big RV, but I hadn't *really* thought through just how difficult those assholes could make it to get out if they weren't challenged by my friends, or the cops, or the military. There's no way you could have made that trip without professional help – and you still lost half of the people who came with you. I'm feeling a little guilty about how easy it was for me to get here. And I understand why you reacted like you did this morning." He paused for a few seconds. "Do you really think you can ever go back? If I was in your shoes, I'd be worried about facing charges for murder if the wrong people were in power. Those guys on the bikes, you said you were in a rural county where that happened. You probably have a warrant out right now if anyone saw your vehicle on that road. They have to know by now that you made it to Canada. Heck, your military escorts blew the hell out of their roadblock and even the Canadians were launching mortars at them. If the U.S. still had any kind of coherent government on June 6th, that would have been an international incident – Canadians shooting at Americans across the border. It's not something that's going to stay a secret no matter how dysfunctional the government is right now."

"I have given prosecution some thought over the last few weeks. If things ever do calm down in the U.S., Canada probably isn't the best place to hide from extradition. It could throw a wrench in an asylum claim if I have a warrant for my arrest, or maybe it would help my claim. I have to hope the Canadians aren't going to send me down for a militia trial just because some crooked prosecutor in a country in the middle of a civil war wants to hang me for protecting my family from fake patriots. I have a pretty damn good self-defense claim if the legal system under the U.S. constitution is still alive, but that's something I can't control. The only witnesses are either dead or were fighting with me, and who knows what the Canadian military did with the gun that matches the bullets. I'm not going to lose any sleep over it right now, too many other things to worry about."

Chad nodded solemnly, "Yeah, I get you. It's not like you could have done anything different. They forced your hand and now you have to spend the rest of your life with it dragging behind you. It sucks."

In the distance some fireworks started going off for Canada Day.

Jim stood up. "I better go check on my kids. First time with fireworks since all the bad happened. They'll probably feel better if I'm with them."

"Sure. Are you leaving tomorrow?"

Jim nodded. "Yeah. We've got an appointment with immigration services in Calgary that I can't miss. It was nice meeting you. Good luck."

Chad stood up and they shook hands before Jim started to walk away.

Chad called out. "Hey, Happy Canada Day."

Jim waved without stopping. "Happy Canada Day...and God Bless America."

Joy was already on top of the situation when Jim stepped into the camper. Kelly was wearing her noise-cancelling headphones and Alex was Deaf. Joy had decided there was no point in doing bedtime until the fireworks were done, so Alex was reading on the couch and Kelly was up in her sleeping area drawing on her iPad. Jim and Joy went into the bedroom to talk.

"So, did you let your new friend know you're leaving tomorrow?"

Jim nodded. "Yep, he's a good listener. I'm going to miss him."

She moved closer and lowered her voice, "Kelly has been working on a comic or graphic novel, whatever you want to call it, on her iPad for months now. I took a look at it while she was in the shower tonight and the story took a very dark turn in the parts she's written lately. Violence, blood, death. I'm really worried about her."

He touched her arm. "Tomorrow we stop playing vacation and start the long path to recovery, for all of us. We'll get there. I guarantee it."

She sat down on the bed. "I really hope that meeting tomorrow goes well. The girls weren't much help in coming up with ideas about where to live. It's a little too abstract for them to grasp until they can see a place. The most important thing is their health right now. I don't even care if they take the year off from school as long as we can get them mental health care and fill their prescriptions."

He sat down next to her, "You should do most of the talking tomorrow. You're so good at getting schools to provide services for the families you work with. You know how to bend bureaucracies to your will and determination. I wouldn't want to be a government official standing between you and medical care for our kids. I'll back you up, but you should do the driving." He gave her a mischievous look. "Just don't get us thrown out of the country."

Joy smiled and elbowed him in the side. "Don't tell me what to do. You're not the boss of me." She stood up. "I think the fireworks are done. We should make them go to bed."

34

July 2 - Outside Calgary

Jim woke up to the birds singing outside the camper again. He pushed the sides of the pillow against his ears to muffle the sound and decided he was going to stay in bed until his alarm went off this morning. Most mornings waking up in the camper, Jim was excited to get out of bed and get the family moving on that day's adventure. Today he was more nervous than excited. Not only were they headed to a meeting that could determine a great deal about his family's immediate future, but they had to get to an office within the city of Calgary.

Driving the RV through a larger city was always an adventure. Jim thought about how uncomfortable the drive into Washington D.C. the previous summer had been. Every lane change was an adventure of honking horns and one-finger salutes from impatient drivers, apparently hurrying to important appointments. The last thirty minutes of that drive was all white-knuckle stress and narrow roads with parked cars on both sides. Jim had mapped the route to the Calgary Immigration Office, and it was near a highway, so there wasn't going to be too much driving on city streets, but the office also didn't seem to have much in the way of RV-friendly parking nearby. He hoped they would be able to find some parking on the street near where they had to go. Worst-case, he would drop off Joy and the girls at the office, find a place to park further away, and walk back to meet with them. They had done this plenty of times before.

Jim lay awake thinking about how the meeting might go. He had always believed that if you didn't have high expectations, you couldn't be disappointed, but today he really hoped Sheila at immigration services would find a way to meet their biggest needs – letting them stay for as long as needed, allowing them to get work permits so they could try to find jobs, and allowing them to get medical care (even if they had to pay for it themselves). If she could help them decide where to go and help them find a place to live, that would be above and beyond. Jim reminded himself to temper his expectations and let Joy do most of the talking when they got the chance to present their case.

Since all he could think about right now were things that caused him stress – the drive into town, parking once they got there, their future in the hands of a bureaucrat – Jim knew his sleep was over. He did his usual morning ritual and slipped outside as quietly as he could. It was shaping up to be another nice, summer day in Alberta. Clear skies and sunshine this morning.

It was almost 7 a.m., so at least the birds had allowed Jim to sleep later than yesterday. He would give the family until 8 before he made them start moving. If they could be on the highway by 9, they could be on the outskirts of Calgary by 10. Then they would find a place to stop and make the day's important phone call. He really hoped they could get in for their meeting late this morning or early this afternoon, but that was out of his control. When he was younger, he had issues with impatience, but since becoming a father to kids with special needs, he had willed himself to learn to be more patient. His girls usually took longer to complete tasks, and he had learned to let them do things at their pace to allow them to have successes. Often, he had to manually override his own impulses, and sometimes his instinct to step in and help took over before his brain could stop it, but he was a more patient person than ten years ago by far. If they had to wait a day or two to get in for their appointment with immigration services, he would accept that and be patient about it.

With about an hour to kill, Jim sat down at the picnic table and pulled out his phone. He had one bar of service, but that should be enough. He opened the Apple News app and typed "Washington Post" into the search. No results. He tried a couple other U.S. news sources – CNN and USA Today – but got no results there either. Giving up on U.S. sources, he scanned the headlines at CBC, The Independent, and The Guardian, but saw nothing related to the U.S. He wasn't expecting anything, but felt the need to try every few days on the off chance someone had found a way to report some news about what was going on back home. The information blackout couldn't last forever.

With nothing to read, Jim decided to see if Chad was outside and maybe get his contact information. If Chad did go back into the U.S. this fall, maybe he would be able to send back some information. Jim hopped up from the picnic table and strode across the road.

Jim found Chad outside his camper, but in the middle of what appeared to be some type of meditation ritual behind his camper with his back to the road. This was new to Jim, and he wasn't sure if he should let Chad know he was here, or if interrupting the meditation was in bad taste. Then Jim wondered if it was rude to even be observing Chad's act of meditation. Maybe it was a really private thing. Not knowing what to do, Jim quietly backed away and walked back to his own campsite. Once there, he dug in the storage compartment and found some scrap paper and a pen. He wrote his name, cell number, and email address on the scrap of paper along with a short note, "nice meeting you, call or email any time."

Jim walked back to Chad's campsite and left the note on the picnic table, held down by a rock. Then he went back to his camper and dumped the tanks one last time, unhooked the waste hose and stored it, pulled out the manual stabilizers and packed them away, and did a walk-around to see if anything else outside needed to be stored away. He would hold off on unplugging the electricity and removing the privacy cover from the windshield, but everything else was packed and ready for driving.

It was not quite 7:30, but Jim decided to try to get the family moving a little early. He really wanted to be on the way to their meeting. When he got inside, Kelly was already awake. She was doing something on her iPad and seemed to be just waiting for Jim to come back.

"Hey dad, are you going to make crepes for breakfast?"

Ah, now Jim understood Kelly's better than normal morning mood and why she wasn't already having breakfast. "Sorry sweetie, the rest of the crepe batter is going to have to wait until we're at our next camping spot. Maybe for supper tonight if mom doesn't make us find a Harvey's in Calgary."

"Ooh, Harvey's. We should have that for supper instead of crepes."

Jim sat down next to Kelly and put his arm around her. "I was thinking that today is a special day for us. So special that I think we should hold off on breakfast until we can find the nearest Tim Horton's. How does a big box of pastries from Tim Horton's sound to you?"

Her face lit up. "I'll go wake up mom and you wake up Alex. I can be ready to go in five minutes."

Jim hugged her tightly, "I think it will take us a little longer to get on the road, but you can go get mom and I'll get Alex moving. As long as I can remember how to sign 'doughnut', I think Alex will be easy to wake up today."

Jim stood up and let Kelly get out of the booth. She hurried back to the bedroom yelling, "Mom, get up, we're going to Tim Horton's."

Jim chuckled knowing Joy was going to have a hard time saying no to that plan now that Kelly was so excited about it. As soon as Joy was awake, Kelly raced past Jim and scampered up into her sleeping area to change out of her PJs and into some clothes.

Jim got Alex moving and after the whole family got themselves cleaned up, dressed, teeth brushed, and other morning rituals taken care of they were ready to go. Jim unhooked the electricity, took the cover off the windshield, packed away the electric cable and the vinyl cover, and they were ready to go.

When Jim got into the driver's seat, the girls were chattering back and forth about what type of doughnuts they hoped to find at the restaurant. Jim hoped they wouldn't have to drive all the way to Calgary to find a Tim Horton's because the girls might not be able to handle that long of a wait. He mapped the route to the nearest restaurant and they headed out of the campground.

After a thirty-minute stop at Tim Horton's where each of the girls put away two of their favorite doughnuts, Jim mapped the route to the immigration office. They would have to stop somewhere along the way and call before they arrived, but Jim wanted to make sure they were taking the best route for a thirty-foot RV, so he zoomed in and made sure it looked doable before they started driving. It was about 8:40, and Jim had to suppress the urge to try to call the immigration office before they got back on the road. Angel had said to call after 9, so he needed to be patient. He decided to drive for another thirty minutes and then start looking for a place to pull off to make the call.

At 9:15, he took an exit and pulled off to the side of the road. He dialed the number on the slip of paper and got an automated voice message. After punching in the extension number on the paper in his hand, he got to Sheila's voicemail message. Voicemail was disappointing, and Jim left a long message explaining who he was and that someone named Brad was going to contact her about getting his family in for an appointment today, if that was possible, or as soon as she had an opening. He left his number and hoped he didn't sound too crazy and desperate on the recording.

Joy was just as disappointed that the call ended with him leaving a message, but they decided to keep heading towards the office and they would detour to the nearest Walmart if they didn't hear back by the time they got to Calgary.

They hadn't gone ten miles before the phone rang. Joy answered it and Jim heard her half of the conversation as she talked excitedly to Sheila about meeting as soon as possible.

"How soon can we be there?" She asked Jim.

"I don't know. You have the phone with the GPS. I think we're about forty-five minutes out."

They agreed to meet at 11:00.

Jim drove straight to the part of town where the office was located and was pleasantly surprised when he found a parking spot less than a block from the building. They had about twenty minutes to kill, so he called a family meeting to go over the game plan.

"Okay, this is a really important meeting for us today. So important that we are going to let mom do most of the talking. Everyone under-stand?" He looked around and got nods of agreement. "You girls need to be on your best behavior. Sit up and only speak when someone asks you something."

Alex raised her hand. "What if we need to use the bathroom? Can we speak then?"

Joy smiled. "Yes, honey. There are exceptions to the rule. Dad just wants us to act like a family that would be good Canadians for as long as we're here. We want to make a good impression. The other rule is that dad doesn't get to sing "Oh, Canada" unless he's ordered to by the Royal Canadian Mounted Police."

Jim tried to look hurt. "As least I know the words. Maybe I can do an interpretive dance about what it means to be Canadian while I recite the song rhythmically. Here, I'll show you." Alex and Joy hurriedly grabbed Jim to stop him from standing up.

"So, back to the serious business," Joy began, "you two should each pick out a book that will keep you occupied in case the meeting runs long. We'll put some bottles of water and some snacks in dad's backpack along with the books."

Jim got up and grabbed his backpack out of the bedroom, dumping everything in it onto the bed. As he returned to the living area, he looked to Joy, "Do you have the birth certificates and passports in your backpack?"

She nodded. "I've got all that plus my ID and the documents they gave us at the bank last month. Is there anything else you can think of that we should grab?"

"Well, if any of you have a secret good-luck charm, you might want to bring it with you. Otherwise, let's all do one last bathroom stop and then head out."

The immigration office was about what Jim expected. Nothing fancy, just simple furnishings, but clean enough. Sheila came out right away and led them to a meeting room with a table large enough to sit all of them. Sheila asked them to explain why they wanted to stay in Canada.

Joy introduced the family and explained their current circumstances. She went into a little detail about what happened back home, what they went through to get to Canada, and how that had affected the girls. Without giving too many details, she talked about what kind of medical help she thought the girls needed. She mentioned the blackout of information coming from the U.S. and the fact that they hadn't been able to reach any of their family or friends back home since they got here. She talked about her fear of running out of money, their need to refill prescriptions, how they had been living in an RV for almost a month, and how they were hoping to be able to settle into some consistency through the coming school year. Finally, she went through her list of what she was hoping to find in the place they settled down. World-class PTSD counseling for teenagers was now the top item on her list, followed by schools, housing, and work.

Jim spoke next. He reminded Sheila that the U.S. border checkpoints weren't currently open so they couldn't drive back even if they wanted to, but they had no desire to go back until they knew it would be safe for their family. Then he explained that even though he had a college degree in business and accounting, he was willing to do any work that was in demand. If there was a community that needed manual labor or a farmhand, he would do his best to learn and perform that job if that would allow them to stay in Canada. He wasn't looking to take a good job from a deserving Canadian, he just wanted to make enough to put a roof over his family's head and food on the table over the next eleven or twelve months until the situation in the U.S. could be understood. At that point, they would need to reevaluate their situation. As he saw it, they were looking for temporary work permits, medical care which they would be willing to pay for if they needed to, and education for the kids. If they could find a community that would provide that for the next year, they were more than willing to work and volunteer in the community.

Sheila then turned to the girls. Kelly had been sitting still so long she was about ready to explode. When given the opportunity to talk, she overshared a bit, but she was honest to a fault. Kelly shared that she wanted her mom and dad to be able to stop worrying about where they were going to live and when they were going to run out of money. She also shared that she wanted her own bedroom and that she wanted to replace all the stuff she had left behind in her room in Minnesota.

Alex spoke last. When Alex talked about how nervous she was that she wouldn't be able to have an interpreter in school who was fluent in American Sign Language, Sheila's demeanor changed from the level of a helpful bureaucrat to that of a fierce advocate.

Sheila had a niece who attended the Manitoba School for the Deaf in Winnipeg, and she turned helping this family with a Deaf daughter into her top mission. Without making any definitive promises, she told them she thought she could help them out if they would be willing to live in Winnipeg. She asked them to give her twenty-four hours to work things out. Could they come back tomorrow at 2:00?

Jim was hopeful and surprised at how the meeting ended. They went back to the RV, all of them a bit stunned by the turn of events. Their prospects seemed positive, but they couldn't know for sure.

Once they got into their seats, Jim opened up his RV park app, found the nearest Walmart that allowed overnight parking, and set the map to get them there.

35

July 3 - Calgary

Their afternoon meeting with Sheila was better than any of them could have expected. She had work permits for Jim and Joy. She had medical cards for the entire family. She had found an apartment complex near the School for the Deaf that had three-bedroom units available. Finally, she had arranged for Jim to interview with an employer looking for warehouse labor about a ten-minute drive from the apartment complex. There was a middle school only a couple blocks from the apartment complex where Kelly could go to school. Winnipeg was a big enough city that there would be good medical facilities to meet their needs. While it hadn't been at the top of their list of places when they talked a couple days earlier, Winnipeg was starting to sound like just what they needed.

Sheila gave them an address in Winnipeg and a phone number and told them they should try to get there in the next few days to look at the available apartment while there was still a three-bedroom unit open. Winnipeg was about thirteen hours away, so they left right away and spent the night of the 3rd at a Walmart in Medicine Hat. Kelly was thrilled. They drove straight to Winnipeg the next morning.

36

July/August - Winnipeg

The family was able to move into the three-bedroom apartment two blocks from the middle school on the outskirts of Winnipeg. They signed a one-year lease on July 4th. Moving into an apartment in Canada was the strangest way they had ever celebrated America's Independence Day. It wasn't a house like Kelly wanted, but she got to have her own room. It was going to take a while to replace all of the toys and books she left behind, and Jim hoped she wouldn't try to hold him to that, because some of those items might be hard to acquire in Canada. They needed to spend their money wisely for the time being.

Jim got hired at the job working in a warehouse; manual labor for low wages, but he was willing to take just about anything that would pay. The owner of the company let Jim store the RV in the back of the property for free, so that was a big convenience. There was no good place to park it near the apartment and Jim was tired of moving it from street to street to avoid getting a parking ticket.

They bought a used Prius to get around town, and Jim thought of Chad just about every time he looked at the car. He hoped Chad found the note with his contact information and wondered if he would get a call or an e-mail someday.

Sheila had set them up with intake appointments for the girls at a clinic in the city that had expertise with children who had been through traumatic events. After the first appointment, they settled on two hours a week of counseling for each of the girls going forward. Jim thought that was too little. He thought maybe daily therapy for a month would cure them, but Joy assured him that the experts knew what they were doing.

The weeks before the start of the school year were a blur of activity. Jim worked weekdays and the girls were able to take public transportation to get to their appointments downtown. In the evenings and weekends, they worked on furnishing their apartment, arranging and re-arranging things continually until everyone could agree on the layout. Jim pulled the TV and DVD player out of the RV and set them up in the living room of their apartment so they wouldn't have to buy new ones – though they rarely got any use. As a family, they explored the neighborhood and figured out where to do the shopping and where to find restaurants that had food that everyone in the family liked. They did the walk to the school a few times at different times of the day so the girls would be used to the streets they would cross. And they stopped in the local parks to see if there were other kids in the girls' age range hanging out there.

As August was coming to a close, the girls began to get nervous about starting at a new school. Kelly had been doing on-line school back in Minnesota and was anxious about being around other kids all day again. In her counseling sessions, Kelly started really letting out her emotions. She would come out of the sessions tear-streaked and exhausted. Alex had decided to stay in the mainstream school, rather than attending the Deaf school, but she was worried about the new school environment and whether she would be able to get a sign language interpreter. She wasn't as emotional as her sister, but she started to act out at bedtime every night. Joy had to assure Jim that the counseling was working, that the girls just needed time to overcome their fear of the new school, but they really were making progress. It didn't feel like progress to Jim, but he was off at work fifty hours a week and had to trust that Joy was seeing progress in the girls' daily lives.

A week before the start of the school year, Jim, Joy, and the girls attended an open house at the school and Joy got the girls registered for classes. They met with the counselor for the girls' grade and Joy explained that in the U.S. the girls both had Individualized Educational Plans (IEPs) and she wanted to make sure they could get similar services in this school. Joy apologized for such late notice, but let the counselor know that Alex would need a sign language interpreter or a captioning device in her classes. They talked through the different technologies that Alex had tested in school over the years and the counselor set up a meeting with herself, Joy, various special education representatives, and the school principal for later in the week.

The meeting with the school officials took place during the day, so Jim was at work and unable to attend. Joy came home with written plans for each of the girls and seemed upbeat about the likelihood that the school would actually come through and implement those plans. In her work, she had seen plenty of school districts agree to written IEPs then completely disregard them, so she was usually in prove-it mode when it came to the plans. Surprisingly, she sounded confident the plans would be followed and she was excited for the start of the school year.

37

September - Winnipeg

With the start of the school year, Jim was expecting some regression in the girls' behavior at home, especially Kelly's. She had never done well with in-person school, and he had been preparing for nightly drama. To Jim's surprise, both girls seemed to be loving their new school environment. They were treated like minor celebrities by some of the other students who learned that they had been through battles with militias to get to Canada. They were brave foreigners who had faced bullets and explosions just a few months ago. Instead of treating Kelly's quirky personality traits as something to bully her for, she was given the leeway to be herself by a small group of friends that became close with her. While she still became overwhelmed at times by the school environment, having friends to support her throughout the day made the days tolerable, sometimes even good.

Alex always did well in school, and after her initial hesitation, she went right back to pushing herself to get good grades. She still had a hard time socializing with the other kids at the middle school, but the School for the Deaf was near their apartment, and she started attending events there on the weekends and an occasional evening. She quickly met some other kids in her age group who signed as well as she did, and her social life took off. Jim would go to pick her up at the Deaf school and he would always have to go into the building to find her and bring her out. She never wanted to leave her friends. He was happy that she had become a social butterfly, but was always embarrassed by his poor communication skills in sign language when he had to try to communicate with other people at the Deaf school.

Joy walked to school with the girls every day and started volunteering at the school during the first week. By the end of the third week, she was offered a part-time, paid position during school hours since she was already there most of the time anyway. Like Jim, she wasn't doing work that her college degree prepared her for, but she was making money and it felt good for her to contribute to the place that was educating her kids.

Once school started, the psychologist made arrangements to see the girls in an office near the school, so Joy and the girls didn't have to travel downtown after school twice a week. Two days a week the girls went straight from school to counseling. On those days Joy would have Jim pick up fast food on his way home from work because she didn't have time to make anything – Harvey's was her favorite, mostly because it doesn't exist in the U.S.

By the end of September their lives were starting to settle into a regular routine of work/school/counseling with some social time for Alex at the Deaf school and Kelly usually spending at least part of Saturday or Sunday hanging out with some of her friend group. The previous June almost seemed like something from a different life except for the mental scars they were carrying around.

Jim was too busy to spend much time thinking about the U.S., but every Sunday he tried to call his mom and his sister from both his Canadian phone and his American phone (which still had service, unbelievably), with none of the calls going through. He also tried various news websites and Apple News with the same results every week – no news out of the U.S. Jim also tried to access his American bank accounts through the app, but that was also unsuccessful. The cell plan must still be getting paid automatically, though, or that phone wouldn't work anymore - unless the cell phone company was so disorganized that they couldn't even shut down unpaid accounts.

One Sunday evening, in late September, Jim and Joy felt confident enough in the girls' progress to leave them alone in the apartment for a couple hours while mom and dad went out on a date night. They hadn't done many date nights since the girls were born. When their daughters were younger, Kelly's need for consistency required one of them to be home for the bedtime rituals and it wasn't easy to find trusted childcare for special needs kids. When the girls got a little older, Jim and Joy would do a date afternoon and go to a movie or for coffee.

This wasn't much of a date, just a nice evening stroll together with a stop for ice cream along the way, but it felt like a huge step in the right direction. There was a little early fall chill in the air, but it was a nice evening. Neither of them felt stressed about having to go to work the next day. Even before the bad stuff that happened that summer, Jim couldn't remember feeling this relaxed and happy about the way their lives were going since the girls were little.

Here they were renting an apartment, and they didn't know if the house they owned was even still standing. They were making a fraction of the income they made back in the U.S. They didn't know if their retirement accounts or other assets in the bank still existed. Yet the last few months had been all about being together as a family, in the here and now. He hadn't felt this close to his daughters in a long time, and the girls hadn't been this happy since they were toddlers.

He and Joy were making enough money each month to pay the bills they incurred each month, so they didn't have to use the money in the bank, but they weren't saving anything either. It was almost like they were taking a year off from thinking about the future. Kelly had been thrilled on Canada Day when she thought this school year was going to be a free year. Jim thought maybe they all needed a free year where they just lived for being together now. They both had lost track of that at some point as they worried about saving for college and retirement and pushing the girls to work on their study habits and do well in school. Jim now realized that both he and Joy had spent way too much of their mental energy stressing about the future.

As they slowly walked back to their apartment holding hands, Jim thought about how lucky he was to have this chance to get his priorities in life straightened out.

38

October - Winnipeg

September rolled into October and their days started to become routine. They would all have breakfast together before Jim left for work, then the ladies would all walk to school together. Jim enjoyed the labor of the work he was doing. He had started to build up some muscles in areas that had atrophied over the years of working behind a desk. The fact that he didn't need to make important decisions and got to leave his work at the warehouse every day at 5:00 was refreshing to him.

Joy was also happy helping out at the school. She liked being there in case either of their girls had an issue, and the work she was doing didn't cause her any stress. She joked with the girls about them pretending they didn't know her when they saw her in the hallway, but they were more likely to yell "Hey mom," if they saw her between classes than they were to pretend they didn't know her.

Kelly had never been happier in her life. Back in the U.S. she had school friends, but nothing like the group of kids she was associating with now. In 6th grade in the U.S., she had been picked on by a few girls and neither she, nor her friends, were equipped to stand up to the bullying. Now her friend group stuck with her even when she said or did something odd. She was with a group of kids that appreciated having someone a little quirky in their group. Every evening she was on the phone or on a video call with at least one of her friends.

Alex wasn't as social at school because there weren't other Deaf kids there and she had trouble following conversations in the school environment, but she still loved going to school every day. Joy repeatedly asked her if she wanted to transfer to the School for the Deaf, but Alex wanted to stay at the mainstream school. She looked forward to the two classes every day that she shared with her sister. Always the over-achiever at school, she worked really hard to get good grades. And though she was coming in seven years late on Canadian history, she put in a good effort in the class and was learning. She kept spending time at the School for the Deaf on the weekends, hanging out with her new friends there. She would have video calls with her friends regularly as well.

Joy made sure they all had dinner together every night and spent some time talking to each other about their day and what they were going to do the next day. Jim went to the store and bought some of their favorite board games and they made a point to have family game time together every weekend. Jim couldn't get into Canadian football, so he had a lot of extra time on the fall weekends to spend with Joy or with whichever one of the girls wasn't busy at any given time. He would borrow the girls' history textbooks so he could learn Canadian history in his free time.

In late October, Jim came home from work one day to find Joy pacing around the kitchen looking nervous. Because that was unusual these days, he immediately got worried. The girls were in their rooms chatting with their friends until dinner time, so they sat down at the table to talk.

Joy started. "My cell phone rang at the school today and I didn't have a chance to answer it. I figured it was you, because who else would be calling me during the work day, so when I got back to my phone I didn't even look at it, I just went to the missed call and called it back."

"I didn't call you today," Jim interrupted, "who was it?"

"It was from my mom's number."

Jim's jaw dropped. "What! Your mom tried to call you. And it got through. Did she leave a message?"

Joy put her phone on the table and played the message. "Joy, its mom.

I hope you're okay and I wish I knew where you were. I'm okay. I'm staying with my sister. I think the worst is over here...." The message cut out.

"Well, that sounded like your mom. Unless its AI generated, it means she's still alive. I'm going to guess your call didn't get through when you called back."

Joy shook her head. "No, it didn't even ring. Maybe she was in a car and drove through an area that had service and just called me real quick."

Jim shook his head. "I don't think so. In the old days if you were out of cell range and someone called you, they could still leave you a message. That's what you did when we first crossed the border in June when you called both of our moms to let them know we were safe. I've been assuming that the reason we couldn't reach anyone in the U.S. is because U.S. carriers have blocked calls originating outside the U.S. and anyone in the U.S. trying to call someone outside the U.S. But somehow her call got through this time, at least for a minute. Maybe the cell company had a glitch and let the call through or maybe someone at the company let it through intentionally. Either way, we know it's possible to reach people in the U.S. Keep your phone handy and hope she gets through again. Have you tried texting her?"

Joy nodded. "Still undeliverable. I tried again about twenty minutes ago."

"I think this is a positive development. Your mom is alive, and she thinks things are getting better. If she was able to call out, maybe other people could as well. Later tonight I'm going to check the news websites to see if there's any reporting out of the U.S."

Joy dabbed at her eyes. "It's great to hear my mom's voice, but it reminds me that she's been stuck there going through who knows what while we've been as happy as we've ever been as a family. I feel guilty about how great our lives have been going lately. I used to talk to my mom almost every day. Now I haven't talked to her in almost six months. I miss her so much, and she's missed six months of the girls' lives. With Thanksgiving and Christmas coming up, I'm going to feel even worse not being able to be with our families."

Jim came over and hugged her. "We had to make the call to save our kids and didn't have time to run across town to go looking for your mom. With my family in Wisconsin, there was no way to reach them. We can't feel guilty for doing what we had to do to keep our kids safe. And remember, half the people who came with us didn't make it. At least your mom is still alive."

"That doesn't make me feel any better right now," she sniffed.

He took her hands. "I know, babe. But do your best to keep your guilty feelings under your hat and let's not talk about this in front of the kids just yet. They are living their best lives right now and I don't want to give them something to worry about."

She nodded. "They are so happy these days. If you would have told me on July 1st that we were going to be this happy four months later, I would have called you a dirty liar. This may not be our forever place, but for now it's really great."

He smiled at her. "Yep. And I sure am glad Sheila didn't make us go to Quebec City. I would have really had a terrible time learning French in my late 40's."

That night after the kids went to bed, Jim sat up for a while searching for any news stories out of the U.S. He found a story from the CBC that said there were reports of American cell phone calls reaching people outside the U.S. for a brief period earlier in the day. The calls were reported around 10:30 a.m. Eastern, and within minutes the connections were cut off. Based on second-hand reports from the people who received the calls, there may be millions of Americans dead since early June and some larger cities may have suffered massive destruction. Some callers said that the military had stopped following the orders of the President and was fighting against militia forces who were backing the President. It was not possible to confirm any of the information being reported by the callers as all social media and news media out of the U.S. is still blocked by the government. It's not known how the calls got through since all cell traffic into and out of the U.S. has been blocked since early June, but Canadians with friends and family in the U.S. are encouraged to continue to try to reach their loved ones on the chance that they might finally get through.

39

∽

November/December - Winnipeg

It was strange not having a four-day weekend in late November. They celebrated Thanksgiving on Saturday instead of Thursday. As a family, they made everyone's favorite dessert and cooked a big dinner together. With no football to watch, they played board games all afternoon when they weren't tending to the food.

Winter in Winnipeg wasn't much different from winter in Minnesota. It snowed; it was cold outside. Jim was kind of enjoying not having to shovel his own driveway for a change. They spent more of their time indoors as the days were shorter and there was less to do outside.

In early December, Jim's boss took him to a Jets game. Jim hadn't been paying attention to what happened with the NHL (he had been a casual fan in the before times), but the Canadian teams were playing with their rosters comprising mostly Canadian, European, and Russian players. The quality of the hockey was still very high, and Jim was happy to see an NHL game again, but it was bittersweet without the American players and teams. Jim couldn't help but wonder about the American players. *How many of them had died since June? Would any of them play a professional hockey game again?* He hadn't been to an NHL game since the North Stars left for Dallas, but if the Wild ever started playing again, he decided he would make a point to go see them.

Christmas was a low-key, family affair. Most of the kids Alex knew at the Deaf school went home for the holidays so she was only seeing them over video calls. Kelly went to the mall with her friends once during school break, but otherwise stayed home with mom. The girls received gifts, but nothing too extravagant. The girls seemed to understand that the family was trying to live on a smaller budget, so they were unusually happy with whatever they unwrapped.

Jim and Joy tried every couple days to text and call back to their relatives in the U.S. throughout this time, but the lines of communication were still down.

Right before the holidays, the psychologist recommended they cut back from two hours a week to one hour a week for each of the girls. They were still benefitting from counseling but didn't seem to need quite as much therapy. They were improving.

40

January to May - Winnipeg

The second half of the school year had its ups and downs. There was drama, as there always is for teenage girls. The girls had a birthday, and, like Christmas, the presents were unimpressive. Jim found a bakery that would make the girls' favorite birthday treats – frosted sugar cookies for Alex and a naked chocolate cake (chocolate cake with no frosting) for Kelly. It wasn't quite as good as their favorite bakery in West Duluth, but the girls appreciated the effort.

Kelly turned in a decent performance at school considering her attitude the previous summer. She got mostly B's and one C. Alex, as usual, worked really hard and got A's in everything, even history.

As the winter snow melted and spring settled in, the news reports that Jim scanned on the weekends started to carry more unverified information from the U.S. that was sourced from people who had crossed the border or who had found ways to communicate to the outside world electronically around the information blockade. Jim still couldn't access the local newspaper in Duluth (if it even existed anymore). The app for his bank in the U.S. still wouldn't open, nor would any of the other U.S. based applications on his phone, but the news reports said that the military was taking control of the country and was in the process of restoring order.

There were still pockets of resistance, and some areas were considered safe havens for the militias, but the military now had control of Washington D.C. Reports said that the Chairman of the Joint Chiefs of Staff had asked the cabinet to invoke the 25th Amendment to remove the President, but many cabinet members resigned immediately after the request was made. The U.S. appeared to be headed to a constitutional crisis since the President, Vice President, and Speaker of the House were all implicated in the violence against American citizens.

It was unclear how the country was going to find a way out since there was still so much chaos and destruction, many members of the minority party in Congress were either dead or missing, and the mid-term elections held the past November were considered illegitimate in much of the world because there had been no voting in the cities that were under siege. The President's party apparently now had a filibuster-proof majority in the Senate and a veto-proof majority in the House. Congress wasn't going to impeach their party's leader, and the cabinet members were resigning to avoid implementing the 25th Amendment, so the only remaining option to remove the President was a military coup.

41

Late May - Winnipeg

The floodgates broke and news from the U.S. started flowing freely the last week of May. Jim moved the TV into the bedroom (so the kids wouldn't be distracted by the news) and spent almost an entire weekend sitting in front of the TV while scrolling news stories on his phone. It was information overload, but he wanted to know everything.

The military ended up storming both the Capitol and the White House and arresting the President, Vice President, many members of Congress, cabinet members, most of the West Wing staff, and leaders within various government agencies who had conspired to make the violence possible. It would likely take years to get to the bottom of the evidence and find all the culprits, but the military police arrested the people they had already accumulated evidence against. By the time the arrests were done, the Secretary of Agriculture was the highest ranked person in the line of succession who had neither resigned from the cabinet, nor been implicated in any criminal actions. He was suddenly sworn in as President of the United States.

Joy spent that weekend trying to call her mom. The media had reported that cell service between the U.S. and Canada would be available, but she wasn't able to get through. Jim wasn't able to reach his family either.

Jim checked on the status of the border stations between Manitoba and Minnesota during that crazy weekend. As of that weekend, they still were not open for cross-border travel.

Jim was glad to go back to work that following Monday. His mind was frazzled from everything he had read and watched, yet he still didn't know anything about how things were in Duluth or how his family in Wisconsin was doing. Spending eight hours doing physical labor was just the thing to get him to stop thinking and worrying about a situation that was out of his control. At the end of the day, he grabbed his stuff out of his locker and saw that he had a missed call on his phone. It was from his sister. He hurried out to the car and called her back.

He probably shouldn't have tried to drive home during the call, but, based on recent history, he wasn't expecting to get through, so he dialed as he was backing out of his parking spot. Amazingly, the phone was ringing. His sister answered as he was pulling out of the parking lot, and he almost forgot he was driving when he heard her voice. They spoke the entire way home. His mom was staying with his sister now. Where she lived, there hadn't been much violence. Some people who worked in their town's government, particularly running elections, had been publicly executed the previous summer, but there hadn't been large-scale power outages, and the militia members who tried to take over the town were eventually driven out by armed citizens. Even with backing from the highest levels of the Federal government, the militia couldn't run the local government and all services fell apart. The town now had a citizen's patrol keeping the streets safe until the government got reorganized and was able to pay the police force again. She didn't know anything about what was going on in Duluth, although she had heard rumors that things got really bad over there during the summer and fall. She hadn't tried to get to Minnesota, but the Bong Bridge was supposed to be open now. There would be checkpoints at both ends to keep troublemakers out, but she had a friend who had crossed the bridge without incident.

Jim let her know his family was safe in Winnipeg and that they were doing well. They arranged to try to do a video call that weekend so the girls could see their grandmother for the first time in a year.

Jim was excited to share the news with Joy when he got into the apartment.

As he entered the kitchen, he saw Joy and the girls sitting tightly together at the table with an iPad in front of them, all talking over each other. As he got closer, he could see Joy's mom on the screen. He ducked in behind them, said hello, and waved. Crazy how much things could change in one day.

42

June 30 - Winnipeg

The month of June had been a busy one. Jim had finally been able to gain access to his bank accounts back in the U.S. Amazingly, the money was still there. His CDs had been rolling over every three months automatically. For now, he would just leave the money there until he knew what they were going to do as a family. Jim was finally able to log into his 401k plan on-line and was not surprised to see that it had dropped in value by over seventy-five percent. So much for the President's platform of being the best candidate for the economy and the stock market. Nothing Jim could do about that right now. He would just leave the funds invested in mutual funds and hope the markets would come back as the country was rebuilt.

Joy was able to access her Facebook account and she had to limit her daily catching up time because it was so heartbreaking. She lost count of the number of people her Facebook friends reported dead over the last year, it was so many. At least fifty people she knew had lost their lives since they left. From the photos that were posted going back to the previous summer and fall, large areas of Duluth had been burned to the ground and the entire complex of government buildings downtown had been firebombed. Piedmont Elementary, where the girls had spent 1st through 5th grade, was totally destroyed along with the shopping center on the same block. It would take years to rebuild the city back to where it was before. It was still too early, and the local government was still too disorganized, to get an accurate number of Duluthians who had died or left since the previous June.

Jim and Joy had spent much of June trying to decide what to do. The borders were open, and Minnesota was thought to be safe for travel, but there were no guarantees. Their RV had been completely repaired earlier in the month, other than the satellite dish which Jim was willing to wait on replacing, but Jim had disposed of the armor from their trip to Canada and they would be travelling without any weapons other than a pocketknife. In the past that wouldn't have been a concern at all, but in their minds the unrest in the U.S. had just ended a month ago. Could everything really be like it was in the before times that quickly? After doing as much research as he could, Jim concluded that much of Northern Minnesota had been like his sister's town. The citizens had taken the towns back from the militias pretty early on, if the militias had even been there. And by now, lots of other people had travelled between Manitoba and Minnesota in the last few weeks and there hadn't been any reports of murdered or missing travelers.

Jim arranged to take some time off around Canada Day and they planned to spend a week at home to see what it would be like if they went back. They didn't renew their lease on the apartment. The landlord let them go month-to-month for now, so they had flexibility. Where they would finally decide to live was still an open issue and he didn't know how long it would take for them to come to that conclusion, but this next week would have a big impact. He was leaning towards spending one more school year in Winnipeg, but they would have to make the final decision as a family.

He had set up the route to use a different border crossing than the one they used to enter Canada. Although he would have loved to see that place again without live ammunition being fired at him, he didn't want to bring up any bad memories the girls might not have worked out in therapy yet.

As the day of their departure approached Jim found that he was more anxious and nervous than excited – the opposite of a normal RV trip. He had loved living in Duluth, but after all that had happened, what would their old neighborhood be like? Had Carl and Julie gone back to their house? Would Norm's family be there waiting for payback? What would happen to Chuck and LeAnn's house now that they're gone? What condition was his house going to be in after a winter without heat?

At 7:00 a.m., Jim hauled the last bag from their apartment to the RV. The girls were all in their regular spots, ready for a long day on the road. For once Jim didn't even have to be the bad guy making everyone get ready for an early departure. It was about a seven-hour drive to Duluth and if they only made a couple of stops, they could be in their old neighborhood by the middle of the afternoon. Joy's mom had verified that their house was still standing, and the girls couldn't wait to go in and see their bedrooms. They also couldn't wait to see their grandmothers and a few other relatives who would be coming to visit for dinner tonight if they got back in time. Some of their cousins were still unaccounted for and hadn't been heard from since the previous June, but this would still be a joyous reunion.

Jim hopped into the driver's seat and turned around to look at his family. Kelly was at the table concentrating on her iPad, headphones in her ears. Alex was on the couch watching a show on her iPad. Joy was in the passenger seat, earbuds in her ears, looking at him and smiling. "Are we all ready to travel to a foreign country today?" He asked.

Silence. Neither of the girls even looked up from their devices.

"Now that's how a family RV trip is supposed to start." He looked right at Joy, "USA here we come."

About The Author

Bill Pank is a Certified Public Accountant from Duluth, Minnesota. He lives with his wife and twin daughters. The Pank family spend their vacation time in a thirty-foot class C motorhome visiting national parks in the U.S. and Canada.

This story was a family affair. Marie drew a sketch of the cover way at the beginning of the process, and listened closely while I read the chapters to her as they were completed. Kealey read the chapters as they were completed and made useful suggestions throughout the process. Allison designed the cover, spine, and back cover using her computer-design skills and offered encouragement throughout the process of writing. I appreciate all of you for your help.

Author's Note

One early morning in June 2022, while I was exploring a campground on Prince Edward Island and listening to Cassidy Hutchinson's testimony to the January 6 Committee, the general plot of this story began to take shape. Jim's early wake-up at the beginning of the story pretty closely matches how that morning started for me. It took another year before any actual writing took place (with some urging from my family). Throughout that year, there were attacks on power infrastructure and foiled plots for more attacks. Armed militia members showed up to peaceful gatherings to intimidate their fellow Americans. Public officials, educators, and medical profession-als received death threats. Bomb threats to schools and swatting calls targeting public figures became a daily feature of living in America.

While I was writing, the 2023 Presidential primary debates took place and some of the candidates said they would use the military to invade Mexico. Some said they would pardon anyone convicted for violence and seditious conspiracy related to January 6, 2021. The former President promised retribution if he returned to office. The scariest things I could come up with to include in this story were actually campaign promises, made on national television, by people aspiring to be Commander-in-Chief.

While I don't know how big the Christian Nationalist movement is in the U.S., I do know that it is antithetical to the message of Jesus in **my** Bible. I think the biggest threat to America right now is home-grown and self-inflicted. We have charismatic demagogues getting rich preaching doom, culture wars, and hate instead of the love of Christ – and too many followers who want to be angry and don't want to hear about "woke" Jesus. When a significant portion of Evangelical Christians say they may need to resort to violence against their fellow Americans to save their country, their definition of Christian doesn't have anything to do with the man the movement was named for anymore.

May God have mercy on all of us.

Thanks for reading.

9 798990 418905